the
rotation

USA Today Best Seller
michel prince

THE ROTATION
Copyright © 2019 by Michel Prince

ISBN: 978-1-68046-858-8

Published by Satin Romance
An Imprint of Melange Books, LLC
White Bear Lake, MN 55110
www.satinromance.com

Published in the United States of America.

Cover Design by Ashley Redbird Designs

For Reggie, who has always understood my stupid ways and accepted them.

CHAPTER ONE

Running down the hallway, trying to get away from my best friend Mark, shouldn't have been so eventful. Sure he was chasing me with a *Super Soaker*, but the worst I expected was a wet ass. Instead as I took the corner going Mach 1 I ran straight into a brick wall.

Okay, so it wasn't a wall, but it felt like one. Unfortunately, it smelled like *Hugo Boss* and made me fall back. But to its credit, the wall reached out and caught my wrist, pulling me back before I landed hard on the floor.

The whole thing probably only took less than five seconds, but those five seconds changed my life forever. His name was Gus Tuckman, but everyone called him Tuck, I was under the delusion that he was an offensive lineman known for protecting the quarterback, later I'd be corrected. The wall in question was his large frame that culminated into a set of abs that you could do more than laundry on. He was massive, standing at least a foot over me with biceps that were bigger than my thighs but that day I learned a lot more about him.

First, over his strong right pectoral muscle was a tattoo of a hawk, I assume, fighting its way out of his chest. There were others, but at the moment it was staring me in the face as it exploded from his sweet caramel colored skin with a dark chocolate nipple in my eye.

Maybe I was hungry, but something about the way he smelled, and his body was formed made me want to lick him. All right why lie. I'd seen him over the last few weeks and had noticed him more times than I'd like to admit.

Never half naked. I didn't think he could look better than he did with his jeans hanging off his hips and a polo shirt. Don't get me wrong he didn't sag his jeans instead he wore them right on his waist so if I had been lucky enough to catch him in a white wife beater I could see the cut of his muscles as they came together to point to something greater beneath his top button.

"You can't escape me," Mark yelled as I felt the cold water hitting the back of my head and Gus's chest causing him to yell out.

"Death wish."

"Oh shit, Tuck, I'm sorry I totally was going after Katie. I never meant—" With that Mark turned and ran for the safety of his room. For the first time I realized I had wrapped my arms around Tuck's waist. I started to let go when one of the defensive lineman Cedric ran down the hall and pulled the towel from Tuck's waist. Tuck's response was to pull my body tight to his covering the now bare front of him. To say it was awkward would be the understatement of the century.

"Don't move," Tuck warned.

"Gotcha," I replied swallowing hard. Why did he have to smell so good?

"Ced—give me the towel back."

"Dude, I'll leave it here for you." He threw it into the phone booth at the end of the hall. "I told you I'd get you."

"I thought you meant on the field."

"Life's a field, baby. Life's a field." With that Cedric took off down the hall.

So here I was holding on to Gus Tuckman trying to preserve a small amount dignity for him. I couldn't tell if it was embarrassment or my desire to see where those abs led that made me want to pull back, but I knew better. Opening a can of worms I wasn't ready for at that moment. Wanted. But not ready for.

Tuck's breathing was even, and he didn't appear to be upset or ashamed. That was my department. The heat in my cheeks made me long for a good second-degree sunburn. At least that would be cooler. Instead I knew I was red, I'd say about one shade under fire truck.

I kept my face forward, but that just allowed the sweet smell of his cologne mixed with some intoxicating sweet smell to invade my nasal cavity. My hands, tight to his back, but I could feel the top to the curve of his ass. Something that I had been observing a little too much lately.

Curiosity is for scientific research not for sexual exploration. Spending your teenage years with an overbearing father you hear it all. It's not like I hadn't done worse with a guy, luckily, when he caught me before the long lecture it was early in my sexual exploration and clothing hadn't been removed.

I digress as I could feel my hands start to slide. Tuck made me jump and reposition my hands in his mid-back.

"I'm Gus by the way," he said looking down at me.

"Katie. So you're a lineman?"

"No, defensive back."

Who was the new lineman everyone was talking about? Okay, normally small talk is hard. With a man who was obviously naked under his towel on the way to the shower standing with your body as a guard it's extremely unsettling. Especially when he's so damn good looking I get fantasies when I see him clothed a hundred yards away.

"So you think we'll win this week?"

To that Gus laughed causing both our bodies to shake so not a good idea.

"I've got a t-shirt on under my sweatshirt how about I…"

"Yes, please. I'm sorry I—wow—" he said nervously.

"It's okay, I watch *Seinfeld*."

"Are you saying something about shrinkage?"

"No, it's just I—Oh man—" Suddenly there was something very large and very hard pressing against my stomach. "I didn't mean to imply…" Well that answers the final question I had about him. I thought you had to buy things that big.

"Now I'm sorry." His voice was a tidge higher than before.

"Felt a breeze, did you?" I joked trying to regain my composure.

"That's all it takes."

"So they say."

"That and the squirming you're doing to get that sweatshirt off isn't helping."

"I'm not used to looking up when I take off my shirt. Never thought of that before. Here." I held out the sweatshirt and he wrapped the fabric around the front of his waist as he walked backward toward the phone booth.

Stepping in he couldn't fit so he just looked at me. "Do you mind?" His finger twirled in a circle.

"Yeah…I gotta go anyway."

I turned taking off down the hall back toward Mark's room. Oh. My. God. I think I just hit fire engine red.

"Marcus Kloski you're so dead," I yelled as I went into his room. "Did you see Ced coming down the hall when you ran?"

"Of course I did. I thought he'd back up Tuck in my annihilation."

"I'm going to assist in your inhalation, loser." I picked up his pillow and beat him repeatedly about his head. "Are you kidding me? That was humiliating."

Mark grabbed me and flipped me to his loveseat sitting on my stomach. We'd been friends since we were toddlers and became best friends in middle school, after a failed attempt at dating for two whole weeks in seventh grade. People couldn't understand how we could stay friends, but that's what seventh grade dating is for. Setting up your future best friends. You never kiss, you may hold hands and you tell them everything because you're in love.

Luckily for me Mark weighed only about one sixty and his six-foot frame made him a twig. He was the normal preppy guy with the perfectly quaffed blondish brown hair styled to look windblown, but I knew how much product he goes through to look 'natural'. The only thing that made him different from anyone else in our class were his dimples.

I don't know how a guy that had absolutely no body fat and even less muscle had a fat face with dimples. Either way he was adorable especially when the light would catch his hazel eyes with the small specs of green in them and his slightly crooked nose. It's not like he couldn't have gotten it fixed years ago, but he said it makes him look tough.

Truthfully his nose was broken in the car accident that killed his parents. The one thing about him I know a hundred percent is that he'd never fix that nose of his no matter how much his stupid girlfriend bugs him to do it.

"Oh, come on you ran into some guy. You get his digits? You were gone forever."

"That's what happens when a guy loses his towel in the middle of the hallway and uses my body as a fig leaf."

"Seriously?"

"Yes, dickwad, now get off me before I pee my pants on your couch." I shoved on his back making his bony little butt dig into my gut.

"You know some would see that as an idle threat."

"But you know better." I started slapping him until he began to move.

Content with his torture of me, Mark got up and crossed to his beanbag. "So was he naked?" he asked drawing out the word naked and accenting it like an SNL character.

"And happy to see me."

"No!"

"Yes, jerk off."

"You gonna hit it?"

"Shut up."

Mark was the only guy who actually had a vague idea of who I was sleeping with. A few guys tried to say I had been with them, but they'd never say it to my face. Mark always wondered why the guys I slept with never admitted it. He liked to say I was so bad they blocked it out. I say I stunned them into silence. Plus they knew they'd never get a second shot if they ran their mouths.

"Is he what women find attractive?" he queried as he flexed his pathetic muscles.

"Tall, dark and handsome? No, we go for chicken legs like yourself. Don't you know I only keep you around to feed my deepest, darkest fantasies?"

"I know where the bodies are buried, but a hand job would make it so I kept quiet."

"Too late. Missed your chance."

"Come on, you know it turns you on."

"If I wanted something small and hard, I'd suck on a Jolly Rancher."

"See now you've upped it."

I don't know why he even joked about sexual favors. We had crossed that bridge long ago and not only decided against it when we realized it skived both of us out. But for some reason we still liked to tease each other. If nothing else, it kept everyone else guessing. Mark might as well be my brother. Come to think of it messing with one of my brothers wouldn't be as disgusting to me since all but one were practically strangers to me anyway.

Bringing my hands to my face in an attempt to bury the thoughts brought Tuck back to me. The smell of *Hugo Boss* mixed what could have only been the most amazing sweat smell created from a human had left its trace on my hands.

That made me remember my digits had been clinging to his hips and back. I couldn't help remembering the feel of the soft skin that surprised me. The pads of my fingers recognized a two-inch scar at the top of his pelvic bone. Maybe a keloid scar. It was smoother than his skin more like silk to satin. All of it made me warm and I had an itch I needed to scratch.

"What do you know about him?"

"Him who?" Mark asked while flipping through channels hoping to find something of interest.

I glared at Mark; he knew me better than that. He smiled at me and leaned back.

"You are interested. He must have had a very strong showing."

"Yes. Yes. Now dish. You know the boys dorm is more of a gossip mill than the women's any day."

"Men's dorm," he corrected. "And yes, it is. I can report that he has a steady stream of visitors and phone calls in any given night. He's a transfer student from some Ju-Co and he's supposed to be the best end on the team. But I don't know if that's his position or a body part description. Now, my bestie..." he said sliding his hand up my leg.

"How many years will I have to say no before you stop?" I asked leaning in toward him as he sat on his knees looking at me like a lion to a gazelle.

"I shouldn't have screamed like a girl in seventh grade."

"Told you, you had your chance. It's too bad you were so stupid you had to find out from Todd that you missed the time of your life."

"Why did you jackoff Todd?" Mark asked, doing a backwards tuck and roll, landing in front of his bed.

"He started it."

"If your daddy knew about you...."

"I get A's and I'm not picking up the latest antibiotic, so he's happy."

"Are you?"

"Always. I'm living life without regrets. Speaking of which, I have a friend to see and a paper to write."

"Who is it tonight?"

"I'll never tell, and neither will he." I kissed Mark on the forehead and headed for the stairs to see if my friend on the second floor was around.

CHAPTER TWO

Chance had been in love with Samantha since ever. I took off the *for* it had been so long. Samantha has been dating Dave for as long as Chance had been in love with Samantha. You see the obvious problem. I'm his solution and he's mine. Well, one of mine.

I found out my first year here every guy I was attracted to was in love with some other girl. Not dating, but completely twitterpated. At the time I was put off, but then I realized I wasn't looking for long term I was looking for right now. So the few guys I found that weren't already in love got relegated to the same treatment.

As my father said, *you're going to college to learn, not to get married.* Taking my father's advice, and twisting it for my own needs, I decided I'd scratch an itch when I had one and keep myself separated from the situation. It was critical I learned to separate myself from emotional attachment if I was ever going to be a doctor. At least that's what my father says. *You cannot get attached, Katherine. Those who get attached find themselves burning out in a few years.*

Knocking on Chance's door, hoping he could scratch the itch Tuck had started, I couldn't help remembering his form. God he was gorgeous. Strong jaw. Hell, strong everything.

"Hey, Katie, what's up?" Chance wasn't bad himself. Tall, blond, blue eyes all the classic surfer looks in a pretty good basketball player. His long hair was great to run my fingers through. He was a Polo Sport wearer. Another in my top ten smells.

"I was heading home, but I was thinking I wanted something to dream about."

"Cute."

"So, is your roommate coming home soon?"

"Probably not until curfew. He's got someone in your dorm. Come on in. Hey where's your escort?"

"Recovering from me kicking his ass."

"Mark?"

"Yep. He thought a *Super Soaker* was the way to go."

"I don't get you two."

"He's the brother I never wanted."

In actuality I liked the little bit I knew about my brothers, but Chance didn't even know I had siblings. That would have been way too much personal info divulged. Chance pulled off his shirt and cleared his bed. We had long ago moved past the formality of seduction. I was there when he needed me, and he was there when I needed him.

"Before you I didn't think I could truly be friends with a girl."

"Mark's not a friend like we're friends." Chance understood he wasn't the only one I randomly slept with, but outside of saying who I wasn't with, he didn't know the other men, and I don't think he cared.

I dug through his desk drawer to find his stash of condoms.

"You were thinking about me." I joked holding the extra sensitive brand that claimed to be ribbed for my pleasure.

"You are constantly on my brain. Twenty-four-seven."

"Liar."

"It sounded good." Wrapping his arms around me he kissed me as we moved into our regular routine.

An hour and two condoms later Tuck had left the forefront of my mind. To my surprise he was actually still in there, propped up on a folding chair in the back corner of my brain, taunting me with his firm—

"What if I wanted you to stay?" Chance asked catching me off guard.

"Since when?" I asked pulling on my tennis shoes.

Chance lay on his bed, propped up by his elbow and wrapped in his dark blue comforter.

"Did someone get engaged?"

"No...not yet," he replied with irritation.

"Then why feign the attachment."

"Such big words," he joked wrapping his free arm around my waist and pulling me to him.

"Feign is only five letters." I tugged on his wrist and freed myself from his hold. "No really?"

"I don't know, maybe Samantha isn't all I thought she was."

"I call bullshit. Our arrangement is fine with me." Taking his chin between my thumb and index finger I lightly kissed his lips. "I don't want to pretend to be yours knowing all too well I'd never be her."

I was under no illusion part of what drew Chance to me was the fact I was probably only a half-inch shorter than Sam. We both have oval faces, although hers was minus the juvenile freckles sprinkled across my nose. Both our eyes are grey, and the shade of our brown hair is identical. Although hers is more luxurious and seemed to shine like the sun off of a calm lake. Mine was flat. Finally, she has the chest, I have the ass, but I know to Chance there's enough for him to imagine her when he's with me. I could almost feel the change in him when he floated into his fantasy world.

"Who are you thinking about?"

"Only you." Leaning over I snagged another kiss.

"My turn to call bullshit."

"I gotta go, I got a micro test this week."

"Micro as in small?"

"Microbiology."

"Brain."

"Jock."

"Hey, could you type something for me?"

"It'll cost you."

"Pizza or chicken?"

"Surprise me."

"You're my best friend ever."

"Ah the euphoria of sexual gratification."

He dug through his backpack to find his paper while I marveled at his chiseled body with only a pair of boxers on. Oh, I knew what was underneath, but still there was always an air of mystery when a man wore boxers.

"Here, it's on Plato's theories."

"Deep," I said grabbing his poorly written mess of a paper. Scribbles and chicken scratch. He's lucky I can read doctor, or I'd never be able to translate this. I wouldn't rewrite it, just spell check and he knew that. If he wanted more, he'd have to take it to the students who charged cash, not food on a weekend when the café closed early.

Looking in the mirror above his sink I smoothed out my mousy brown hair and judged how much longer the flush would be in my cheeks. I'm known for leaving guys' rooms, but at least as far as I know not being thought of as anything more than a tutor. I'm surprised how people didn't make that connection. My ability to pick the right guys gave me a little bit of pride. The men were gentlemen enough to not go in for the locker room talk, which kept me a mystery to most on campus.

"Katie, you are like one of the guys."

I rolled my eyes at the comment I'd heard a thousand times. Looking down at my jeans and t-shirt I wasn't surprised they thought that.

"Did you have a coat or something?"

Shit my sweatshirt. And Tuck's back. I'm sure Chance asked because he cared, but damn it I don't have time for another round to throw Tuck to the back of my mind if not completely out of it where he belongs.

"I wasn't thinking when I came over tonight. It was kinda warm," I lied.

"You want to borrow one of mine?"

"No thanks." Evidence that he was more than my tutee? Not in this lifetime. I opened his door and grabbed my bag. "When's the paper due?"

"Monday."

"Good I'll have it by Saturday." I looked at the eight page scribbled mess and changed my mind. "Sunday. One of these days—"

"I know, I know I'll learn how to write." A few guys passed by us but didn't even notice me. Being plain I found if I didn't engage someone in conversation, I could go completely unnoticed. It has been that way my whole life. Like I'm Ms. Invisible, how I feared the movie *Home Alone* because I knew forgetting me was a reality. If I had a nickel for every time I heard, *Oh I didn't see you there*. I'd be a millionaire.

CHAPTER THREE

I had a fitful sleep, which wasn't odd for me. The reasoning was. When I reached for my pillow to hold tight, I remembered holding tight to Tuck. When I wasn't holding on to something I couldn't get to sleep. Ugh. By 5:00 a.m. I gave up and decided to go for a run.

Pulling on some warm-ups, sports bra and t-shirt I stretched and stuck my key card in my pocket.

St. Justice College was located in a medium sized town in Southern Illinois. Cassen was conservative in most of its practices and mirrored by the college. Sports wise we were only Division III so we were a smaller, with our two dorms built in the early eighties each had six stories. Our campus consisted of a union, admin building, field house, library and five buildings each having a specialty. I practically lived in McArthur, the science building.

Running by myself in the city would have been scary, but in this town, it was calming. Going out the side door I cut through the campus on a route I had created my first year. About two blocks past the campus I felt like I was being followed. Something very unnerving and unexpected. Glancing over my shoulder I saw a dark figure jogging behind me about half a block away.

I wasn't scared, necessarily, because he seemed to be wearing workout gear and wasn't trying to catch up to me. The form looked familiar, but I couldn't place it. Slowing my pace seemed like a mistake, but I couldn't help myself.

Pulling back one of my headphones I could finally hear the sounds of the morning. Birds waking, the last of the night going to bed and a few stray cars going on their way.

"Katie?" The voice was deep, not that I was surprised by the size of the man, but I still wasn't a hundred percent on who it was so I stopped. Okay, so that's the way every good slasher movie starts out and I know better. As he ran under the dimming streetlight, I saw Tuck was my pursuer.

"Tuck?" I questioned as he slowed to a stop by me.

"It's not safe to run on your own."

"Only since I got a stalker this morning."

"I run every morning."

"By yourself. That's not safe," I scolded like a mother.

"Funny, how far are you going?"

"About three miles."

"You want to cut that in half and I'll join you?"

"Sure. You have a route?"

"I think so."

We crossed the street and continued on our run. Not that I minded having protection, but I was confused because he saw me and talked to me.

Tucking my stray headphone into my bra strap I kept the other one wrapped around my ear. I didn't want to be rude, but if he didn't want to talk the last thing I needed was to read too much into this jog. I'm just running with a guy that had me tossing and turning all night because I was imagining him on top of me, behind me, hell all over me.

Plus we're running, it's not like you talk while you run.

"Did you start as a freshman?" Okay maybe I don't know the rules when it comes to shared exercise routines.

"No I started around five."

"What?" Dumb jock, too bad. "I meant at St. Justice, not the run." Okay maybe not too dumb.

"Everyone starts as a freshman."

"Are you always a smart ass?"

"Nervous habit, but yes I've been here since freshman year, I guess. I took college classes in high school so I was kinda a sophomore."

"That's why you're called the brain?"

"I have a nickname?"

"Sort of…"

Okay he wasn't telling me everything. The silence came back, and we kept going for a few more blocks.

"So you're only nineteen?"

He can add, I'll give him that. Not that it ever mattered when I saw a body like his, talking wasn't important. Brains only came in play on the off chance I wanted to marry in a decade or two.

"Yes."

We ran through downtown and cut past the hospital. He turned left and I followed suit. The sidewalk was older and cracked on the next few blocks so I shifted to run on the grass. He followed, but there wasn't much space, our arms touched, and a shot ran through me hitting every nerve in my body.

Katherine Alice you know that's not possible. It would take an electric current or multiple stimulation points. That was my father's way of explaining to me the love described in movies and books could never happen. So sure I knew deep down logically the fact that I'm sure I have two rock hard areolas in my bra and I'm warming in places I shouldn't be was not because the incredibly handsome, fit, perfect jaw line with muscles that I want to lick—stop it. The last thing I need is to take a chance with a stupid jock that can't follow my rules.

"You taken any classes from Snyder?"

Oh, that explains it. He wants a real tutor.

"One."

"Who's her favorite author?"

"Why?"

"I'm trying to decide which book to write my deconstruction on."

The deconstruction assignment is Snyder's way of feeling important. You had to deconstruct a published author's work to show all the flaws. Weighted at fifty percent of the grade in American Lit, I'd seen more than one melt down over it in the last year.

"She quotes Thoreau all the time," I offered. "But Emerson is her favorite so she hides that."

"Because she wants everyone to dissect Emerson and ignore Thoreau since she's not an expert in him?"

Damn it, why'd he have to have a brain with that body? Ugh I hate college sometimes. Just when I think I can protect myself and use a man for sex, he has to peak my interested in a deeper area.

"Personally, I chose Whittier," I stated.

"Since he dissects Thoreau in most of his writing?"

Okay, I officially want him and that is not good.

"Yes. Um—you want to blow her mind and make it so she can't mess with you?"

"Of course."

"You ever heard of William Lynch?"

He slowed down and came to a stop.

"Hear me out," I said with my hands up in surrender.

How the hell did I find a football player with a brain? That's harder than finding a botanist with a personality. That's it. I can't sleep with him. Damn, what a waste.

His face seemed upset at me and I could see his tongue pressing against his canine tooth. Now I was torn. That tongue looked like it could do some wonderful things, but this action was obviously his way of not snapping on me.

"You already know what to do. His speech was published, and that speech caused more damage—"

"So because I'm black I should play the race card?"

"Focus on the man verses woman part."

"What?"

Now we were walking.

"Who raised you?" My clinical evaluation running through my brain.

"My mother and father."

"Together or separately?"

"I'm a black man who was raised in a traditional home. Mom and Dad married then they conceived me." He sneered.

"Well I'm a spoiled white girl whose father's been married four times and my family tree has more branches on my generation than Jonestown had victims," I snapped back. "I was trying to prove a point about Lynch's damage. Find someone—I think I know who, but I'll have to ask him if he'd be willing to talk to you about it. Being male raised by a single mother constantly being told and overhearing how useless and unnecessary men are. Heck just watch *Maury* for a week— look for a while I was raised by my dad and mom, but my mom was totally dependent on him. Even when he left to go to work, she couldn't—I tend to be—" I turned to him and decided that I couldn't go any further. I was rambling and unable to find an answer. "Forget it."

"I want to know. Tell me your tendencies."

"I don't know you."

"Augustus Tuckman, born and raised in Glasgow, Kentucky. Just transferred from Bowling Green Tech. Middle son of Clarence and Sonya. I just learned I should wear boxers to the shower."

"Now who's the smart ass? And that's not a necessity," I added remembering how nice his bare skin felt against my hands.

"Tell me your tendencies. Did you go against your mother like most girls do or did she damage you enough that you follow suit?"

"What time is it?"

"What are you avoiding?"

"Nothing." I took my phone off my arm and checked the time. "Where are we?"

"I thought you were leading."

"Not funny."

"Who's being funny?"

"Come on, Tuck."

"Katie, I'm serious. You're the one that's lived here for a year."

"I have an eight o'clock class and I still need to shower." Somehow, we'd been out for almost two hours. "We had to have run like twelve miles."

"We walked quite a bit."

"Tuck, tell me where we are." Panic sunk in twisting my gut. Getting lost is great in stupid romantic comedies, but I can't handle it. I get the shakes and freak out. That's why I pushed to be on the small campus. Even in our Highland Park neighborhood I never ventured out. My hands started to shake, and my mind raced. "Calm down. It's okay. Calm down," I whispered to myself as I squatted down and held tight to my knees. Where's a paper bag when you need one?

"Katie—Katie are you okay?"

Rocking I tried to soothe myself. Then the mumbles started. "You have an hour. This town isn't that big. What did we pass?"

Tuck placed his hand between my shoulder blades, and I started to bite my bottom lip.

"No dirt roads, we're still in town."

"Katie we're on the back side of campus. You know by that one park. They take all the new people here during orientation."

Tuck was talking, but I couldn't calm my brain enough to process. Two hours? We could have made it to Stanford by then. I run a six-minute mile walk ten-minute mile. How long did I walk versus run?

Tuck placed his hand under my chin and pulled my head up so I could look him in the eye.

"You okay." His sable colored eyes were soft and assuring. It was like he had all the answers to the major questions in the world.

"No. I—I—I don't like be—be—be—being lost." I stuttered, our eyes stayed locked and a calm came over me.

"This is more than don't like."

"I got lost once. At a park. It took five hours for the police to find me. My mother and I showed up at the end of the picnic with my family and everyone was staring at me. They were so mad because I ruined it. I don't like being late either. But I never skip class. I have class in an hour."

My panic had caused me to verbally vomit all over myself and unfortunately this stranger was here to get splashed with some of the spray. I could hear myself telling me to shut up, but I couldn't stop sharing these intimate details with him.

"We're like five minutes from your dorm. I have a great sense of direction and it usually only takes me once to know where I'm going."

"Swear." My voice was almost a whine as I tried to understand why I had let myself fall into this trap. *Because you trust him.* I couldn't. Not this fast. But then again, my gut has only failed me once. That was when I let my heart get in the way of it and if I was truthful with myself, I never trusted Clark either.

"I swear. I wouldn't have joked around if I'd known."

He pulled me up and held my hand as we walked back to campus. When I could see the outline of my dorm my heart rate dropped and I finally relaxed.

"Please don't tell anyone I'm this big of a freak. I don't usually talk that much about me—I'm not even sure what I—"

"I wouldn't call you a freak. You're more highly strung. Freak you can't fix. Highly strung can be loosened and restrung correctly."

"Now you're going to fix me." *Please.* I kept my face as straight as I could without considering my body was still a little shaky.

"I don't see much that needs repair." He let go of my hand as we closed in on the campus.

"Thanks for protecting me on my run."

"It was payback for keeping my dignity intact. *Seinfeld* was right, it gets cold in those hallways," he joked dropping his voice an octave and leaning close. I swear I could feel his breath brush against my neck causing me to have a full body shiver.

When he walked toward his dorm I called out, "Hey Tuck."

He turned and looked at me, he said, "Yes."

"Hawthorne's always good too. The victimization of women, the whole double standard thing with Hester. Snyder eats that stuff up."

"Thanks, Katie—hey what's your last name?"

"Gills."

"Thanks KG." KG. He officially saw me as a dude A pal, a buddy. That's okay. He was a major distraction that would get me off track.

CHAPTER FOUR

S howering and rushing to class I made it with only two minutes to spare. For me way too late. Anatomy and Physiology. Today we get our cats. Although we had partners, they were for consult only we each had to dissect our own.

"I've laid out the cats assigned to you. When you remove the plastic the smell of formaldehyde can be very overwhelming so the windows are open. For the next three weeks we will be meeting in the lab instead of the lecture hall. With ten minutes left in the class you will need to clean up and place your cat into the fridge at the back of the lab. Any questions?"

Dr. Kane was a middle-aged professor, and I think he came here because he wouldn't be expected to get published. He did know the curriculum he just didn't really like the annoyance of repeating it to those that couldn't understand. His dark brown hair was always unkempt with his half-rimmed glasses holding it back unless he was reading.

I found my orange striped cat had white paws. Completely stretched out on it's back like it had been jumping and got frozen in mid leap. Mark's was white with black spots or black with white spots depending on how you're looking at it. He was seated across from me.

Cutting open the top of my plastic bag I gagged a little. I've always hated the smell of formaldehyde, but I saw it as a necessary evil.

"Come on, Doc, you can't do that," Mark teased.

"I didn't do it when I cut her open, I can gag at nasty smells."

"Like draining infected pustules?"

"Saying it like that makes me think you're jealous of my future success."

"Come on be a nurse with me." Mark winked.

"Digital impaction removals?" I laughed. "No thanks."

"You had to go there didn't you," Mark said scrunching his nose.

"I know what you look forward to. Speaking of which what's up with Carrie?"

The scrunch turned into a glare. Carrie was Mark's current significant other. They met over the summer when he was asked to make contact with a few of the new students that lived in the Chicago area so they wouldn't have to be nervous coming to campus. She honed in on him right away.

"She thinks you hate her. I wonder why?" Mark twirled his scalpel absently until my right eyebrow rose.

"I'm telling you if you pull the corncob out of her ass her personality will improve greatly."

Carrie had the uncanny ability to follow every trend not really caring if they made sense or not. I'm sure in elementary school she had multiple pairs of jelly shoes, parachute pants and slap bracelets in every color. She had Mark wearing a stupid key while she wore the heart pendent with a key cut out of it. Now I'm gagging for another reason.

I pulled out my packet of identification pins and started to separate them out. Thankfully I had them color-coded. Red for muscle, blue for nerves, green for major organs, orange for tendons and ligaments, and purple for major vessels.

"Anal much?"

I looked at Mark's pile of pins, no flags yet just a plastic packet of pins. Maybe I am becoming too much like my dad. Everything in order and ready to go. Smiling at him I shook my head.

"No, really, how long did that take you?"

"A few hours. I was bored watching a movie."

"Will you be bored tonight?"

"Ask me after Calc Theories. You know Dr. DeAmontie likes to give a chapter a night."

Washing my hands in the small sink attached to the table I patted them dry then grabbed my gloves that snapped as I pulled them on making Mark shake his head. I pulled out my dissection kit grasping the scalpel it caught the light it was so sharp and clean.

"The cat's already dead you didn't need to sterilize it."

"Are you going to be useful at all?"

"Am I ever? Are you over being mad at me?"

"Yes." That run-walk this morning with Tuck was amazing. I wouldn't have had that interaction without Mark's stupid attack.

"You weren't at breakfast this morning." Mark's focus moved away from his cat and to me. "Did you track down a new prey?"

"I went for a run that went long. Don't worry, grandma, I grabbed a cereal bar." Puncturing the skin of the specimen with my scalpel my incision began at the base of the jaw going straight down until I reached the top of the cat's nipples at her the mid point of her abdomen. A clear yellowish fluid seeped out onto the tray. "You think I should name it? Pumpkin or Ms. Whiskers."

I continued to work, slicing along the throat and at the abdominal wall to create flaps.

"You're twisted." Holding the scalpel up I turned to Mark whose jaw had dropped.

"What? It's a dead animal, I thought maybe it would be good to personalize it."

"Okay Buffalo Bill."

"We're supposed to skin it to get to the layers."

"It rubs the lotion on the skin," Mark said in his nastiest voice.

"Is there a problem, Mr. Kloski?" Dr. Kane asked as he made rounds.

"No sir."

"Then I suggest you talk less and do more. You should have at least the chest cavity exposed and labeling started by ten thirty."

"Would it make more sense to expose the lower abdomen after we've completed the chest because of drying out?" I asked.

"Yes, Ms. Gills. I see that you stopped at the diaphragm. That is the smartest way to maintain the formaldehyde. I do have a small saw when you start working on the cranial nerves."

"Will you be grading as we go? So once I've finished the front, I can flip over without doing damage to my work."

"There is very little on the back side. I usually allow the spinal column to be done along the side of the tray without you actually having to dissect it. But if you are ahead, I will allow you to explore."

"Thank you, sir." He walked to the next table as Mark continued.

"It rubs the lotion on the skin or else it gets the hose—"

"Do you want your pins done?" I cracked while holding my scalpel tip close to Mark's nose.

"Yes please."

"Then get to work."

The next hour I had marked all of the larger parts that were necessary. Lungs, heart, esophagus, each of the separate compartments of the heart, a dozen little flags stuck out of my cat that I chose to name Mittens. I'd never had a pet before, maybe I am twisted having my first pet be a cadaver cat.

CHAPTER FIVE

The cafeteria for the campus was located in the student union. The large spiral staircase led to an open sitting area where we all gathered until the doors opened. I found a two-seat, hard couch I heard was made by inmates at the state prison three towns over. They weren't stylish, comfortable or even normal size. The fabric itched and the steel frames were great for posture, but not when I was tired from lack of sleep.

With at least five minutes until the door opened, I snatched my history book to review the two chapters that had been assigned. Then pulled out a swizzle stick from my front pocket and began twisting it around my finger as I read. A hand slid across my shoulders causing me to glance up.

Tuck stood above me with a strange look on his face. He sat in a chair next to me and leaned in.

"I thought you would have showered."

"I did shower," I snipped, then pulled on my shirt and sniffed. The smell of formaldehyde was still stuck in my nose.

"Try again."

"Do you think I care what you think?" Twisting the swizzle stick tighter turned my finger a dark purple before I released and let the blood rush back into the digit.

"Yes." Damn he's right. "I'm just looking out for you. I'd hate for you to lose out on a great guy because you smell like death."

"Not sweat?"

"You don't smell like you did this morning."

"You were smelling me?"

Why did it seem weird when he did it when I would love to sniff him all day long? Breathing in his strong manly scent that seems to add to his cologne as opposed to the other way around.

He smiled and stretched out not answering my question.

"I can't smell because my morning lab had a ton of formaldehyde in it."

"I thought it was familiar." His head turned when there was a loud noise. "Door's open. You running tomorrow?"

"I don't know. I run when I can't sleep," I replied, stuffing my textbook into my backpack and slinging it over my left shoulder.

"You're in too good of shape. Do you have a problem sleeping?"

He pegged me. I was lucky if I got eight hours once a week. Usually I only get three to four a night.

"How about I'll give you till a quarter after if you want to run with me?"

We walked toward the line curling around the hall.

"Are you going to get me lost again?"

"I was thinking about doing a case study for Behavior Therapies."

"I thought you said I wasn't a freak."

"Did I say anything about Abnormal Psych?"

"You think you can cure me?"

"Depends. Will you lay down on a couch and let me do what's necessary?"

My dormant parts came alive. His voice, delivery and general presence had heat rushing through my veins.

"Wow, that was smooth."

"It's a gift."

I swiped my card and got in the hot food line. Looking at the breaded chicken sandwich and French fries I realized I probably should have had one of my in house lunches.

Mark, Bryan, and Gary were already sitting at my normal table. I dropped my tray and headed to the salad bar.

"Katie." Kermit's voice caught me off guard.

His name alone should have been enough to keep him out of my line up, but he wasn't a little scrawny guy. He was a baseball player. First base with arms like Jose Consaqaco, minus the steroid dick. We had been in a few history classes together. He was just like me. Following in the path that was laid out for him without questioning the reason why. An education major with coaching as a minor. His goal. Be a high school civics teacher and coach baseball. His mother is to blame for his stupid name. His father was to blame for the most perfect brown eyes and tanned skin from his Hispanic heritage.

"What's up?" I asked. It had been a few weeks since I'd seen him.

"Any chance you and I could watch a movie this weekend?"

Another of my rules, only on the weekends. I didn't like interrupting my studying and something about the guys seeing me during the week was too close to a relationship.

"I'm not sure." Why did I say that? Just then I looked up and saw Tuck on the other side of the salad bar. That's why I said that. He had already started to infiltrate my thoughts. Stupid images would flash through my mind of him and me in an embrace. The worst were the thoughts of us talking.

My want to know more about him was too much for me. It wasn't like Kermit or Chance. They were merely talented bodies that found mine satisfactory for their immediate needs. Tuck was more than that and that was why I was scared. Treading into a place I had been before only to come out scared. I wasn't about to allow that to happen again. I refuse to be like Mark, falling in and out of love. He says he learns from each relationship, but I can't see it. All I see is my friend in pain when it's over, no matter who ends it.

"Come on, Katie, I miss your…" He looked around and noticed quite a few people were at the salad bar. "*Mystery Science Theater* skills."

"I gotta type a paper, but that shouldn't take all day. How about after the football game?"

I'd need Kermit after watching Tuck for four quarters. Right now, watching him reach for the cucumbers has me enthralled. The way his muscles tense then release in his hands, forearm up to—*Look away.*

"Why you wasting your time—"

"On a real sport," I challenged.

"Hey now, I'll make you watch *Field of Dreams* again."

"And now I'm busy."

"*Major League.*"

"Getting warmer. I'll call you." That was enough to satisfy him, and he walked back to his table. At the drink station I got another visitor. I've got too many balls in the air. I definitely can't add Tuck.

"So that guy?" Tuck asked trapping me by the chocolate milk. For some reason the milk is in the back corner next to a wall. All Tuck had to do is stand at an angle and I had a brick wall, milk dispenser and him with no escape.

The sick part happened when an image flashed through my head of him picking me up and setting me on the counter. His body pressed against mine as the hard wall held us both up. I could instantly feel the heat in my face and a few other places.

"What guy?"

I prayed he thought the blush in my skin was from his question. It wasn't, my mind was still playing out the scenario in my head as he took a step forward making me have to back up. The hard bricks were pressing against my shirt and I could feel it digging in turning me on more.

"The one at your table that likes to hunt you."

Whew, he meant Mark. "Mark." That killed the sexual fantasies in my head.

"Boyfriend?"

"No, Jackie. I keep him around to make me feel smart."

"So you and him aren't…" His fingers wiggled back and forth.

"Into sign language?"

"Together?"

"He was the first of my failures. Alas, I haven't gotten over him."

"When did you go out?"

"Seventh grade. Twelve was a hard year for me."

"Scarring."

"To say the least."

"That's good I'd worry about you with a guy who'd leave you in the company of a half naked strange man."

Mark knows better than to get between a half naked man and me, I thought.

"He would be a bit of a pussy, wouldn't he?"

"To say the least."

"Can I go now?" I stepped to the side only to have Tuck put his arm up locking me in.

"Sorry, I didn't mean to hold you back."

His eyes were amazing and had trapped me completely. I bit at my lips to stop the tingling sensation that had started to get out of control from the second he stepped closer. His lips were amazing. Full, but not large. Dark but with a hint of red underneath when he pressed them together.

"My crappy sandwich is getting cold."

"I'd hate to keep you from food poisoning." He dropped his arm and I slid past him.

"Thank you."

"What about the other guy?" he asked causing me to stop in my tracks. I turned and smiled at him.

"What other guy?"

He leaned in close and whispered in my ear. "The guy you're sleeping with in the salad bar line."

A chill shot through me. *Recover. Recover. Recover.*

"Did I have sex while getting my apple slices? Happens every time. That's it, I'm switching to cottage cheese." I walked away feeling that I had hopefully eluded that situation.

Damn, Kermit, I should have run him over like the toad he is.

CHAPTER SIX

"Katie Gills," the intercom system squawked my name so I took off to the button in the hallway.

"Yes."

"You have an escort."

You'd think two years from the twenty first century they would have updated this antiquated system, but they haven't. It must be Mark. Escort means male. Visitor means female. At least when I go to the men's dorm, I'm a visitor and not an escort

"Okay." Locking my dorm room, I went to the lobby to get him. I don't know why they thought the policy would keep men away from the girl's rooms, but hey it made my dad happy.

Walking down the stairs I turned into the lobby to see Tuck standing by a pillar. I searched for Mark, but Tuck was the only guy in the lobby. He turned around and smiled at me. In his hand was my sweatshirt.

"I figured you'd want it washed before I gave it back." He figured wrong as I loved the smell of *Hugo Boss*.

"Thank you," I said, confused.

We stood looking at each other as if something should have been said between us, but couldn't be. I wasn't sure how to read him. Over the years I'd gotten good at reading people. I was always the pursuer. Not with him.

Mark tells me that guys are afraid of me because I'm standoffish. I console myself in that I've been with some of the hottest guys on campus. Being invisible to most people makes it easy to be free to live my life my way.

I had watched Chance from afar for a while before I approached him. Something about the way his body moved enthralled me.

Then there was 'the mouth'. His real name is Albert. Talk about your misnomers. Al had this way of talking that could entrance a kid with ADHD. It wasn't what he said, but how his lips moved. They were slightly askew. His voice was deep and gravelly like Christian Slater. He could read the back of a shampoo bottle and get me wet.

All the guys in my rotation say the same thing to me at one point or another. *I've never seen you before.* I may have had a half-dozen classes with them, but I never so much as caught their eyes for a second. Sitting back observing the landscape I strike when I see prey I want.

But here, with Tuck, I'm confused. Yes, I'd run into him, but I could have sat on Kermit's lap and wiggled, and he still wouldn't have noticed me if I hadn't been so forward with him. Telling him what he wanted to hear at that moment.

Tuck should not have seen me. That run the morning after talking to me. That doesn't happen.

"Um, did you want to come up?" I asked breaking the tension hopefully between us.

"Yes."

I turned back to the hallway and took the short flight up to my room. Down the hallway I noticed that a few girls gave me a glare so I walked faster.

"This is it."

Tuck plopped down on my futon and messed with the legs of my loft.

"Do you really sleep up there?"

"Yep."

"What about when you have guys over?"

"Guys can't spend the night."

"You know what I mean."

"The weight limit's three hundred so I try to avoid that situation."

Is he fishing for info on my sex life?

"All the time?" He smiled and I had to return it.

"What's going on?"

"Nothing. Just seeing how the other half lives. Girls usually come to my room. I'm not one to venture out."

"So I should be honored?"

"Most definitely. What were you doing? Did I interrupt anything?" His eyes scanned the knickknacks along my windowsill.

"Watching a movie and researching prostitution during the Victorian age."

"Seriously?"

"Seriously. It's for a paper. I hate when people try to put out how bad we are nowadays. The per capita prostitution rate was higher during the Victorian age, and everyone acts like they are the standard of morality. During the Civil War you had to register because the STD rate was so high especially among soldiers and most of the first children born to the Pilgrims were born seven months after the happy couple was married even though they ended up weighing between six to nine pounds."

"Are you into historical sex?"

"History's just a side passion I'm kinda a Biochem major that's really pre-med. They actually go hand in hand when you think of the research behind epidemics and root causes for disease."

"You're going to be a doctor. That's cool."

"No, that's expected."

"You don't want to be a doctor?" He picked up one of my swizzle stick men.

"I don't know what I want. But I'm supposed to be a doctor."

"Who made that choice?"

"My dad. He's a surgeon."

"Do you like cutting people open?"

"Never had the pleasure, but dissection is cool. I don't know if I could do it with the heart and lungs moving."

"What field you looking at?"

"What's with the twenty questions?" I asked with my arms crossed as I stood opposite him. My fingers were twitching wanting him to return my little stick figure to its right and proper place.

"You've seen me naked." He placed the figure back then plopped down on my futon. Outstretching his arms, he rested them on the back of my futon. "I get a few questions."

"Correction. I saw you with your shirt off…and felt what you'd look like naked."

"I think that's worse."

"I guess I'm in trouble. You mind if I get comfortable."

"How comfortable?" he asked, the question rolling off is tongue is such a way I couldn't help but get the double entendre.

"Well, I usually sit around my room in a bra and thong just in case a pillow fight breaks out."

"High heels with the fluffy feathers on them?"

"So you're my peeping Tom."

"Gus, but you can call me Tuck."

We spent the next two hours talking with me moving from my overstuffed chair to the futon and by the end of the night he was rubbing my feet while making me laugh harder than I had in a long time.

"Exactly how many of those things do you make a day?" he asked as I finished the latest in my swizzle stickman army.

"Nervous habit. I need my fingers busy and my father used to ply me with Shirley Temples while he worked the room at a conference."

"Nerves or boredom? Because if I'm boring you—"

"A little of both I guess. Depends on the situation."

"How did you trick me into this?" he asked looking at my foot in his hand. "I didn't even know I had started doing it."

"I have you trained already. That's not a good thing for you."

We were watching *Nick at Night*. *The Addams Family* was on and I had to laugh. Morticia had just spoken French and Gomez was all over her as usual.

"I never got how that was supposed to be a turn on," I mused.

"What? The arm kissing or the speaking French?"

"Both really, but how is someone kissing your arm a turn on?" I asked glancing at him. I got the sudden feeling I had thrown down a challenge. His dark sable colored eyes started to sparkle even though the light hadn't changed.

"If I may?" he asked holding my hand in his. "Would you please?"

"No."

"*Pas.*" He corrected with the worst French accent ever. "Just one little word. *Oui. Rouge. La Glass.* I'm out of French words please *ma chere.*"

"French toast," I said in the most American way I could.

"Oh, you spoke French." His accent was even worse than before. I was waiting for the Gomez attack on my arm. Instead his lips lightly brushed my knuckles. Then another light brush against the back of my hand. I could already feel a tingling up my spine. By the time his soft lips touched the inside of my wrist I caught a chill.

His other hand worked its way gently across my abdomen until he reached my far hip. Firmly he gripped allowing him to be pressed tight against me.

Flipping my wrist over he kissed the inside of it and a shot ran down my leg. His lips continued their journey hitting my forearm then the bend in my elbow. That's when I stopped breathing. More out of fear of me panting. I had never been more turned on in my life. Three short kisses up the side of my upper arm made me regret not putting on a long sleeve t-shirt. I had to bite my bottom lip to keep myself from moaning.

His fingers tenderly slid under my cami, they brushed delicately against my smooth skin. He stayed above my waist gingerly stroking me bringing about gooseflesh along my side.

By the time he hit my shoulder I was done. My fingers were dug into my thighs in an attempt to not rip his shirt off and take him for all he would give. All my strength was being used to hold my head up instead of letting it drop back against the wall.

With a light brush of his fingers my hair fell behind my shoulder clearing a path for him to my neck. First three stops on my collarbone, one that included a light circling with his tongue, triggering wet heat between my thighs. He had more than proved his point when he hit my neck and started to suck lightly on my skin.

When his lips reached my earlobe, he gently tugged it with his teeth, a light whisper flowed across my ear asking me. "Do you know anymore French?"

I was just about to start singing *Frere Jacque* when a knock on my door made me jump.

"Sorry," I said pushing my hands on his chest.

He smiled and his tongue glided along his bottom lip.

"Yes?" I called to the door or maybe I was saying it to him at that moment. I wasn't sure. Tuck had me questioning the basics of life.

"Katie, I've got what you need." It was Chance. Damn, it was Sunday wasn't it. Shit, I forgot to print out the paper. Breathing in deep and smelled the fried chicken through the door. Score. Oh no. I can't have Tuck see Chance or vice versa. Chance had played the game long enough to know how to play it, but Tuck...Tuck wasn't anything, yet.

"Boyfriend?"

"No. Why are you so concerned about me having a boyfriend? I don't do the serious boyfriend crap, okay." I jumped up and headed for my computer to push print before I opened the door.

"I'm so sorry, Chance, I just started to print it."

"I was at Sam's and thought I'd stop by on my way home. I can chill for a minute. Hey? I wasn't interrupting anything was I?"

"No, don't be silly," I said taking the bag and inspecting the contents. "You got me sides."

"I had a coupon."

"Impressive." My printer beeped. "Wait, is this cold chicken?"

"No, Dave called when I got up here."

"Dicey. Um, Chance, have you met Tuck?"

"Seen him in the halls, but never had the pleasure." Chance reached to shake his hand as I gathered the pages to pass to him. "Well I guess I better go."

"So soon?" I didn't want to sound excited, but I had enjoyed the foot massage among other things.

"I'm sure Sam's almost done talking."

"Right, see you around."

"Not if I see you first," he teased.

"That's such a bad line." I knitted my brows together.

"I know. Nice to meet you Tuck."

"You too. Hey, Chance can you answer a question for me?"

I glared at Tuck begging him not to push it.

"Katie says she doesn't do the boyfriend thing. Do you know what she does?"

Chance looked at me and started to rock back on his heels. "You want to date her?" Chance asked with an air of skepticism, his thumb hitching toward me.

"Not necessarily, but I don't think people should be alone either."

"I can understand that reasoning. Um, I'm not sure if she's into guys." What a nice recovery. I am going to have to punish him later for that one. "As my friend I'd hate to see her alone too, but I think Katie does what she wants, with who she wants. She's never seemed unhappy to me so I guess I never worried about her being solo."

"Interesting." Tuck seemed satisfied and Chance saw the smile on my face telling him that he did good, but I would get him back for the lesbian jab.

Closing the door, I smiled at Tuck and grabbed the bucket of chicken to share. "Hungry?"

"Sure. Who's Chance?"

"A friend, he can't type for anything so I help him out and he buys me chicken or pizza. It's stupid, but I feel weird charging my friends for stuff that I'd probably do for free if I had the time."

"What type of friend?"

"He's in love with Sam if that puts it into perspective." I dug through the bag to find the biscuits and avoid the conversation.

"Katie, I want to be straight with you."

"Last time you were I got poked in the stomach."

"Funny."

"I try. I fail most of the time, but I do try."

"I don't want anything serious, but I'd like to—"

"Put me in a rotation of booty calls."

"You're blunt. Is that what Chance meant about what you want with who you want?"

"I've been on campus long enough to know there isn't a guy here who's serious. But I respect that you are honest."

"Man hater?"

"Chance is incorrect about my sexual orientation. I've found most guys have a twisted lesbian fantasy."

I opened the warm biscuits and started to dig in. Popping a bit off letting it slide past my teeth sucking on my finger hoping that it could take away the desire I had for Tuck. It didn't. I looked at Tuck and considered his offer.

"Why?"

"Why what?"

"Why do you want me to be a booty call?" I needed to make sure my rep was still intact. Also, I was curious about who, if anyone, had already claimed his heart. I'm not sure I could handle being his backup like I was for Chance. Chance had never made me anything more than curious. Tuck made me want everything and then some. That alone should have scratched him off the list of viable men.

"I like your ass."

I curved my body enough to get a good view. My hand glided from the top of my hip under my ass grabbing it slightly. I could hear Tuck breathe in deep causing my lip to curl up. I liked when a man desired me. It was almost better than sex, because if they desired me that meant they actually saw me.

"There are better ones on campus."

"That's one girl's opinion."

Tuck's legs extended as he leaned back getting more comfortable. Crossing his arms, I could feel his eyes outlining my body. He was drinking me in, causing a heat betwixt my legs. Even though he was sitting across the room I could feel the sexual tension growing stronger between us.

"It's more than that, I didn't want to show my hand."

"I like your hands," I replied raising my right eyebrow and tilting my head.

We were dancing around the subject as I wasn't sure that I could control myself with him.

"Our run the other day and you were really fun tonight. You seem cool and laid back."

"Was this a date?"

"No. More of a fact-finding mission." He slid a swizzle stick from my stash on top of my mini-fridge.

"And I do it for you?" I placed another bit of the biscuit in my mouth allowing my finger to linger. It's not that I didn't know what guys like to look at, I just wasn't one to do it all the time unless I wanted him in my rotation. The sad part was I wasn't trying to be on my tiptoes to accentuate my ass. I wasn't trying to suck on my finger or bite on my lips.

Tuck was bringing out the temptress in me even though I had

thought she had been put away long ago. None of my current men had caused me to subconsciously use what little God had given me. I was getting nervous and flustered but trying to stay composed.

"Yes. On many levels."

"Just not the serious one."

"You said you don't do the boyfriend thing," he replied a little rebuffed.

"But if I did?"

He quit fiddling with my swizzle stick and bit it like a toothpick.

"I probably wouldn't mess with you." My heart tightened around the knife Tuck had plunged into it. This is why I had a rotation. No attachment no feeling.

I sat by him. His hand wrapped around my waist pulling me so I had to straddle his hips. Below me his growing excitement pressed against me.

"Hello."

I plucked my now destroyed swizzle stick from his teeth and tossed it in the trash.

"Hi." I smiled at him and licked my lips. "Honored as I would be to have you in my rotation and being your back up. I'm not sure right now."

"How many do you have in your rotation?" he asked.

"How many do you?"

"Touché." His fingers dug into my hips.

"French doesn't get me going like it does you."

"It's just I guess I never thought about girls having a rotation."

"If a girl's in yours why wouldn't you be part of hers? Or do they have to pine away waiting for when you are ready to give them a bone?"

Recognition danced across his face as he shook his head. "You just blew my whole world away."

"I'm good at that. You want a thigh or a leg?"

"No breasts?"

"I don't like white meat." The moment it fell from my lips I knew what would be coming.

"Then we should get along great."

"That was bad."

"You said it." He raised his eyebrow. "Thigh, please. Unless you want to give me more."

"Not today," I replied sliding off him and sitting back on my futon.

"That's not a no."

"No, its not," I quipped reaching for the chicken only to have him stop me. He took my head into his hands. His body towered over me as he straddled my waist this time.

"Kiss me." His velvet voice flowed past those perfect lips of his.

"No." I smiled too much at the thought of it.

"Kiss me." His lips were brushing against mine causing me to tremble.

"No." My voice barely above a whisper.

"Why not?"

"I'm afraid I won't stop."

"That's not persuasive."

"You're weakening me."

His lips hit mine and instantly every nerve in my body came alive. Heat filled my face, and everything felt right. Too right. He made it clear to me what he wants. Not that I didn't want that too, but I already knew I needed more and sleeping with him would make it worse on me. I refused to become the pathetic goober I was in high school thinking sex was love.

Since I came to college, I'd been good about that. Keeping myself separated, but he was different. I didn't know why and that frightened me more.

His tongue lightly touched mine as his fingers glided from my cheek to the back of my hair cradling my head in his hand. My muscles melted against the back of the futon.

"Can I come by tomorrow?"

"Huh?" I was still stunned by the best kiss I'd ever received in my life.

"Tomorrow? You doing anything?"

"Probably working on the paper you distracted me from tonight."

"After practice how about I come over here?"

"Why?"

"Just trying to work myself into your rotation," he replied as his lips brushed against mine. "What's the schedule like?"

"I have a question for you."

"Uh huh."

"The girl back home in your rotation, do you preplan her schedule?"

"Who says—"

"Don't bullshit a bullshitter."

"You need to stop, or this could get serious," he growled.

"Stop what? I will make sure that I stop it immediately."

"Being so damn cool."

"Fine let's do this and get it over with before you try to attach." Or I attach.

"Seriously?"

"No," I said trying to push him away, but not finding enough resolve to even start.

He wouldn't let me go and I decided to use this time to figure out what I would be getting if he got traded to my team. His hand lightly stroked against my neck as he kissed me in a way that wasn't standard sex-required kiss. It seemed like it was real, confusing me even more.

"Stop."

"I don't think you mean that?" He nuzzled against my collarbone, making waves shoot through my body.

"I don't do the seduction thing well."

"I disagree." His hand traveled up my spine making me catch my breath again.

"It changes me so please don't."

"You like being in control, don't you?"

"Depends." I leaned my elbows on his shoulders. "Do you like being controlled?"

"What are you?" he asked with a smirk.

"The girl that everyone wants in theory, but not in reality."

"Who hurt you?"

I kissed him and decided screw it. If I did anymore talking with him my heart would break. My hands went under his shirt feeling his firm muscles and I started to unbutton his jeans.

"No. Not tonight. Not like this," Tuck said, pulling away.

"Fine. I only offer once." Pushing him to the side I was a little put off, but that was my ego not anything more. Once free I got up.

"Get back here."

"No."

Tuck stood and crossed over to me by my closet pinning me against the door. "I want you."

"I only need to be told no once."

"You told me no, then changed your mind."

"I said not now, not no. Plus I'm a girl."

"I've noticed." His voice was low as his finger lightly traced along my neck running down my chest. It traced the neckline of the cami I wore outlining my breasts as gooseflesh erupted up and down my body. "Tell me the truth. Why weren't you nervous on our run even though you didn't know where we were going? That doesn't make sense if you don't like getting lost."

"It doesn't make sense."

His finger kept its path going up my shoulder finding the strap of my cami and wrapping it around his finger keeping it tight just like he had done to me. At this moment I was locked into him. Every part of my skin was erect and hypersensitive. Even the light whispers that came from his dark full lips allowed breath to brush across my skin making it so I couldn't move without crumbling to the floor.

"No, it doesn't." His lips were but a breath away from mine our noses touching in such a delicate way you would think they had nothing between them.

"Not what you said, but how I feel about you," I replied hoping that he couldn't see my lips trembling or hear it in my voice.

"You have feelings for me?" His finger pushed the strap down my arm, but his eyes stayed on mine.

"I know I shouldn't, but I trust you."

"Doesn't that have to be earned?" he asked leaning to the side allowing our cheeks to caress each other.

"I told you it doesn't make sense." I tried to focus on his supraspinatus, but it didn't work. I didn't care what the muscle groups were, I just wanted them around me.

"What are your rules?"

"Nobody knows what we do, we always use protection and we don't discuss other people we're with. There are more, but right now I can't remember them." I could feel my eyes fluttering as I leaned down trying to hide myself. *Separate. Separate. Sep—*

"How many more?"

"Two or three." Twenty-five.

"I'll accept one more."

"I'm not flexible on my rules. It's all or nothing."

"I'll accept one more." His firm tone made my nipples harden further and burn against the fabric of my bra.

If I think you're attaching, I'm out. If I think I'm attaching, you're out. No sleepovers, they lead to attachment. If he'll only accept one more rule…any of these are necessary. Say it. Say it. The calm sane part of my brain yelled. Unfortunately, Tuck's finger was gliding down the side of my arm and his lips were on the crook of my neck.

"Only on the weekends." Not a steadfast rule, just a general policy that doesn't even really need to be added since homework usually negates interaction during the week. Especially with athletes. Oh God I should runaway from him right now. My nipples are hard, my panties are getting wet and it's taking every ounce of self control to not unbutton his pants with my teeth. The worst part is even if he didn't want to sleep with me, I'd still want him to stay and talk. Oh Gawd, I want him.

"Sunday count as a weekend?" he asked.

"It does today."

"Where's your protection?"

"Top drawer."

"Should I get it?"

"Yes."

CHAPTER SEVEN

Going to the union for lunch I was actually excited. The thought Tuck was somewhere in that building had me tapping my pencil in annoyance as the seconds ticked away in Calculus.

Finally released from class I cross campus only to be stuck behind a group of meanderers. I never wanted to seem eager, but Tuck was all I could think about. Stuck behind poky and the boys the realization I should cut to the dorm instead and eat lunch in my room hit me. The group in front of me veered off and I caught a flash of Tuck holding the door open for a girl at the union. She smiled at him and he returned the favor walking in behind her.

A vice held tight to my chest and I turned toward the dorm.

"Katie. Food. Now." It was Mark.

"I was going to eat in my room."

"No." He wrapped his hand around mine and pulled me to the union. "I didn't see you at breakfast and I need to see you eat at least twice a day."

"Single white male stalking laws are on the books," I advised.

"You and I both know why, now come feed yourself. It will please me in ways you'll never understand."

Trudging into the union I could feel the dread of seeing Tuck with a girl coming over me. Chance saw me in the lobby giving me a head nod while rubbing Sam's shoulders. I acknowledged with a smile and realized I could care less that Chance was touching another girl.

"I gotta go," I said to Mark turning only to have him wrap his arms around my waist yanking me to the end of the line.

"What is up?"

From my vantage point I had a clear view of Tuck sitting next to a girl. She was leaning over resting her arms on her knee. Giggles came from his area and noticed there were three other girls surrounding him.

"I fucked up."

"Katie, it's okay. Calm down. We'll eat lunch and everything will be all right."

"I'm under control," I snapped.

"I didn't say anything about being in control."

"You didn't? Well, anyway—"

"Are you going to be okay?" He placed the back of his hand on my forehead and then checked my glands along my neck. I slapped away his hands, turned around and crossed my arms.

"Who is he?"

I kept my mouth shut.

"Is it a class?"

I scoffed. The line started to move. I saw Tuck get up to join in the line as we walked slowly. Mark's hands pressed on my shoulders and he leaned on me like I was going to carry him.

"I need to know why you aren't feeling good, sweetie. Something has you off kilter."

"I'll be fine if you drop it." Running my ID through the scanner I grabbed a tray. Taking what was given to me I went to the table and started to eat.

"Drink?" he asked.

"White Russian."

"I can't get you Alexei Nemov, how many times must I tell you that?"

If nothing else the thought of Alexei flipping through the air and his muscles flexing as he held the iron cross two years ago at the Atlanta games was enough to get me to smile.

"There's my girl. How about milk? It does a body good."

"Yes, please goofy." He took off and I picked at my peas.

"I missed you at my bad movies of the eighties marathon," Kermit said as he sat across from me.

"Sorry," I apologized and placed my hand on his that were intertwined with each other. "I got caught up with some homework." Really, I didn't want to sleep with Kermit while my mind was focused completely on Tuck. I felt like I'd be cheating on him.

"I miss you, Katie."

"I know." I dropped my head to the table feeling exhausted for the first time juggling men.

"You didn't say me too." Kermit pulled his hands back and leaned against the back of his chair. Glancing up I knew he was pulling out of my rotation. "This is how it ends, huh. It was fun while it lasted."

"I'm going through some stuff right now. I don't feel like myself."

"How 'bout I don't close the door quite yet, but I know it'll be awhile before you stop by."

That's why I liked the guys in my rotation. We all went through highs and lows. "There's something different about you, Katie. Are you sure it isn't something more?"

"No," I said shaking my head. Mark returned with my milk and Kermit took his cue to leave.

"You're still helping him?"

"He was thanking me for last year." I assured him.

Gary and Bryan came and sat in their usually spots. You'd think being in college we'd fall out of the high school routine of grouping at tables, but every day it was the same group of people. Mark was the talker that made the others join. Although I might say something once in a while, I was not who they came to see.

Turning my head, I caught sight of Tuck at the football table. Well, one of them. He seemed to be the center at that table. They were loud and laughing making me afraid he was talking about me.

How stupid could I have been to sleep with him? There was no way he'd follow my rules. But that wasn't what was killing me.

I wanted to be sitting next to him. I wanted to be in the conversation. I wanted him. I wanted to be his. Turning back to my food I kept picking at it.

"Eat," Mark ordered.

"This is not food," I grumbled. I tried to sniff it, but all I could smell was grease and burnt bread. Out of nowhere the smell of *Hugo Boss* overpowered all of the other smells around me.

"Katie, we're friends, right?" Tuck asked as he pulled an abandoned chair from the table next to us.

Friends. Acquaintances. But the smile on his face made me think and I glanced around to see if anyone noticed him talking to me.

"We're friendly." I could feel my face flushed remembering his kiss and the feel of his body on top of mine. The way he would brush his lips across my nipples and his hands found spots ignored by all the rest.

"You do favors for your friends."

"Within reason."

"I need a ride to The Discount Mart."

Damn, I wanted him to ask me to forget that stupid weekend rule I put into place.

"What time?"

"Before practice?"

"I don't have a class until two so as long as you can get done by then I'll take you."

"Couldn't help hearing you needed a ride?" Lana came by and Tuck's face dropped. "My class schedule isn't an issue. You could keep me out as long as you wanted to."

"Thanks, Lana," Tuck replied and drummed his hands on the table. "Sorry to bother you, Katie."

I pursed my lips and started to bite my bottom lip.

"We done here?" I asked Mark and grabbed my tray.

"You didn't eat—" I glared at Mark and he got the message. Not the time. "Your cake, can I have it?"

"As long as you eat it as we leave."

Mark snatched the cake and we walked to the tray line.

"He's the reason you fucked up, huh?"

"Not going to talk about it. I need a nap."

"Katie." Mark's voice was strained.

"Mark, I went for a run this morning I need a nap," I lied.

Leaving the union Tuck caught up to me outside the dorm.

"Katie, I wanted to go with you, but I didn't know how that worked in your rules system."

"It's not a big deal. We're friends, nothing more, so I can use the time to study."

"Where were you this morning? I thought you'd go for a run with me." Lana walked in between us like I wasn't even there. Curling her fingers around the collar of Tuck's shirt she pulled him close.

"Let me grab my keys and I'll be right out."

Scoffing I turned my head away and held back the urge to inflict pain. When she was through the door, I pivoted to him.

"We can't be friends," I stated plainly and turned.

"Wait—why?"

"Because your other friends don't play by my rules."

"Maybe you should run for student council since you seem to want to impose your rules on everyone."

"Not everyone. Just the ones I have to deal with."

"You don't have to deal with me."

"Then I won't."

"Fine, you got your hat, get your coat."

I left him outside as I cut up to my room trying not to speed up my pace. Anything to make me think no one could see that I was crushed inside. Crash landing in my chair I started to pick with the split ends that had taken over my hair as I stared into nothingness.

"Katie Gills." My name echoed from the intercom.

Pushing up I walked to the hallway.

"Yes."

"You have an escort."

"Tell Mark I'm trying to nap."

"It's not Mark." Tuck's voice boomed over the speaker.

"What do you want?"

"A ride to *Discount Mart.*"

"I thought you had a ride to *Discount Mart.*"

"Excuse me. Are you coming down or not? We're not going to do this over the intercom," the front desk girl snipped.

"Fine."

I went to the lobby and stood with my arms crossed.

"Lana has a tiny hatchback. I'm abnormally large. Do you have a bigger vehicle?"

"An SUV. My dad's all about safety." Even I could hear the annoyance in my voice.

"Are we still friends or are you tired of dealing with me?"

I let out a gust of air from my lungs and rolled my eyes so Tuck leaned in.

"The way you moan when I'm deep inside you makes me hard just from the memory of it."

I was always one for flattery. The chill bumps returned as my body warmed. How he could make me have two opposite reactions at once was beyond me.

"I'll take you."

"What was that?" he asked. "You mumble a lot."

"I'll take you."

"Hmmmm?"

"I'll take you. I'll take you. I'll take you." Each statement was louder and caused me to laugh.

"You don't have to beg."

"I hate you. You know that, right?"

"Got the feeling. Let's go."

"I gotta get my keys." He followed me to my room closing the door behind us.

"I hate your rules."

His arms wrapped around me. His lips finding mine, followed by his tongue. In one swift move he lifted me, and my legs wrapped around his hips as the papers on my desk scattered.

"You still need to go to The Discount Mart?" I gasped.

"Yes. I needed a little make out time too."

"I'm sure that Lana would have helped with that need."

"I like yours better."

"You've kissed her?"

"What was that rule of yours?" he questioned with a quirked brow.

"You started the conversation. Never mind, you're right. We need to get out of here if I'm going to get to class on time."

Tuck captured my lips for one last, long, lingering kiss. "You need a minute?" he asked. "You're a little flushed."

"You don't say."

Walking to my car Tuck kept an appropriate distance from me. We were like any other students going to the store. When I pulled out of the parking lot and was officially off campus Tuck placed his hand on mine. It had been resting on the gearshift and he took it off intertwining our fingers while resting it on his leg.

"What are you doing?"

"No one can see us." He had a point, but holding his hand felt so good I couldn't help but feel like this was right. "Don't worry, I won't hold your hand in the store," he groaned.

"If you think I'm such a bitch why do you put up with me? There has to be an easier way to get laid."

"What if it's not about getting laid?" I pulled my hand away and turned my car into the parking lot. Putting the car in park Tuck decided to bail out. "It's nice to have someone to talk to about more than sports."

"We talk about sports?"

"And books, movies, music, classes."

I got out of the car and started to walk into the store.

"You don't talk to anyone about those things?"

"Yes, but you have a better ass than Cedric."

"You're right. I thought all black guys had good asses until I saw him."

"Does that mean I have a nice ass?" he teased as we walked toward the toiletries.

"Good doesn't describe it," I said under my breath.

"Mumbler."

We kept walking as Tuck grabbed the usual stuff. Deodorant, toothpaste, a twelve pack of soap and razors.

"It's amazing you ran out of everything at once."

"Close to amazing." I followed where he walked until in my dream state, I discovered we were by the women's lingerie. True, the men's department was on the other side of the aisle, but it was starting to make me nervous looking at the teddies and thongs on display.

"You allow presents instead of cash?"

"I used less than a gallon of gas getting here. This wasn't a burden," I replied as I absently pulled on the sleeves of some sweaters on a rack.

"You're going to be a doctor someday. Do you know how much an hour of your time is worth?"

"I need to get some stuff so I would have come here anyway."

Tuck grabbed a few packs of t-shirts and tossed them into his basket. "Then why haven't you grabbed anything yet?"

"We haven't passed what I needed."

"What do you need?"

"I'll get it when I see it."

"Let me buy you something."

"How 'bout a *Snickers*?" Skipping breakfast and only having a few bites of lunch was catching up to me. My sugar was dropping, the lightheadedness was more than my proximity to Tuck.

He put his hands on my shoulders, turned me around, and leaning down close to my ear, he whispered, "How about something like that?"

"I don't do butt floss."

"Why? I'm not the only one with an amazing ass."

"Fine, you model a pair for me first and I'll let you know what I think."

"Can't blame a guy for trying. That is if you're going to let me stay in your rotation."

"You're in my rotation."

"Good." His hand slid down and cupped mine. We walked up and down a few aisles and I tossed three decks of cards into his basket. "You needed a deck of cards?"

"I only have one, but I love playing canasta, Canadian style. I finally found a few girls who know how to play."

"You're talking to girls? I never see you with girls."

"I don't hang out with a lot of girls, but I've had a few acquaintances. Plus Mark counts as a girl."

"Always?"

"Except for..."

"Seventh grade. How traumatic was that year for you?"

"For him it was the worst."

"When was yours?" he asked dropping a thong in the cart without looking at it.

"How big do you think I am?" I asked pulling out the XL size, turning back around, and placing it on the rack.

"Who says they were for you?"

"I don't think they'd fit you. Are you a chubby chaser?"

"You caught me. I'm a cross dresser, but I can't convert my size well."

"We've been together once—"

"I remember three," he interjected as he brushed my hair back letting his finger softly stroke my cheek causing me to blush.

"In a year if you're still in my rotation you can buy me one."

"Why if?"

"You're a hot property. I'm pretty sure someone will want you exclusively."

"How many have you lost over the years?"

"A few were called up to the show."

"And you don't get jealous? Putting in all that work only to have someone else getting the well-trained man."

"What training? I don't train anything."

"Rule following—"

"Why do you think I mess with athletes? They understand holding isn't allowed, when I call a jump ball, they accept the possession and I'm the ref, ump, side judge all wrapped up in a cute little package. There is nothing I do your coaches haven't already done."

"Only athletes? You've never messed with a band geek or a science nerd."

"Once, and he ruined it for all the rest. Are you almost done?" I asked.

We had been wandering aimlessly through the aisles talking for over thirty minutes not even looking at the merchandise.

"Have you ever skipped a class?" he asked.

"Once in high school."

"That ruined your perfect attendance record and scarred you for life."

"I'm beginning to not like you."

"I play defense, what do you expect?"

"What does playing defense have to do with it?"

"Reading the QB. Assessing how the line is set up and where the receivers are. I'm good at reading people."

"What if I don't want to be read?"

"I think you need to be."

"Why?"

Tuck shook his head and walked toward the checkout. Grabbing a *Snickers,* he put his merchandise on the belt. I picked up a *Dr. Pepper* to add to his 'hill',

The check out lady started scanning the items and looked at the two of us. She was older and wore a disapproving glare. Nerves bubbled in my belly from her stare. Almost as if we had hundreds of dollars of merchandise stuffed in our underwear. My stomach started to knot up when Tuck turned toward me, his smile making me feel relaxed and I ignored her glare. It's not like she was about to interact with Tuck outside of giving him his total.

"Because my new bestie," he said bumping my shoulder. "Scars heal, but you seem to reopen the wounds to make sure they are raw and festering."

"I do not."

"Lies don't become you."

"That'll be thirty-four sixty-two," the annoyed clerk barked, and Tuck pulled out his wallet passing her a few bills. The clerk held them up to the light looking for the security bar. Satisfied she gave Tuck his change and started to ring up my decks of cards.

I pulled out my cash and realized I only had a fifty. Handing the bill to her she entered the dollar amount in her register then gave me my change.

"Why did you do that?" Tuck asked the lady as she placed the bills in my hand.

"Do what, sir?"

"You checked my bills, but not hers? She's just as capable and likely to give you fake bills as me. But no, me, the black guy you check the bills."

He had a point, but it was making my stomach turn and causing me to fall into the invisible mode. A haze formed around the edges of objects.

"What are you saying?"

"I'm saying check all or none of the bills. What'd she give you? A fifty? How does that have a lower rate of forfeiture than a twenty?"

"You need to leave, sir," she sneered.

"You need to check yourself before you wreck yourself."

"Is that a threat?"

"How would that be a threat?"

Wide-eyed I watched unsure of what he meant myself.

"Do I need to call over my manager?"

"Please do," Tuck egged her on.

"Tuck, I need to get to class," I said placing my hand on his arm and he finally turned to me.

"Katie, you saw it didn't you?"

"Yes, I saw it. But I'm invisible to most people. I never noticed it before."

"Well I do. I'm an honors student, have been all my life. Never got so much as a jaywalking ticket," he snapped at the lady.

"My line is backing up sir," she sneered. "Do you mind?"

"You're lucky she has a class." He snarled, wrapped his arm around my waist, held me close and headed for the door.

Part of me wanted to pull away because of my rules, but instead I slid my hand across his abs and held tight to his body. He was cursing under his breath as we walked to my car. Most of it was inaudible, but the last part made me stop and pull away.

"Excuse me?"

"What?"

"I'm white." I held my hand to my chest and drew out the phrase slowly to make sure he understood.

"I know." He stressed the word drawing it out like I had just done. He acted like he hadn't even said anything wrong.

Unlocking my car door, I slid into my seat and turned over the engine. My fingers fumbled in the cup holder until I found a butterscotch round. Popping it in my mouth I tried to will my sugar level up.

Tuck knocked on the passenger window. I kept my eyes forward and my hands gripping the steering wheel so tight my fingers turned the shade of an early snow.

"Katie you going to unlock the door?" Tuck's muffled voice assaulted my ear. "Look I'm sorry. I don't hate all white people okay. It's just a phrase."

"You gonna be calling me a stupid cracker bitch next?"

"Truthfully you think that woman would have pulled that shit if I wasn't black."

"I'm not her," I snapped. "And for you to generalize that way—"

My door opened and I came to the sudden realization Tuck was no longer on my right side.

"I'm sorry I hurt your feelings. You're right. I don't hate all white people. In fact, some of my best friends are white."

I rolled my eyes at him then dropped my head to the steering wheel.

"You have a class to get to and I would appreciate if you would give me a ride to campus. Maybe even one while you skip your class—"

"Don't push it. I haven't forgiven you yet."

"Plus it's Monday, not Friday," he whined.

"Right."

He brought the back of his finger to my cheek and it brushed ever so lightly causing me to calm down and forgive him. The clerk had been wrong. Way wrong, but I liked to live in the corners and nooks of the world. Not challenging it. Tuck may be a little too out there for me outside of my bed.

To stop my hands from shaking I ate half my candy bar before I left the parking lot. I'd learned early to hide my weakness from others, only Mark and possibly the school nurse knew of my diabetes. Driving back to the campus the ride was quiet until Tuck seemed to think it had been too long.

"I don't ask for it, but people will never change if you don't call them on it."

"I was raised that race didn't matter. That's how I see the world."

"You're white. You can see the world like that because for you it doesn't. But I'm black. I can't hide that fact. It's out there. Everyone sees me as a black man."

"That wasn't the first thing I noticed."

"What was the first thing you noticed?"

"Your cologne."

"Not my eyes?" he said leaning his head on my shoulder and batting his long black lashes that curled up in a way that looked soft as a dandelion. "Come now, Katie…tell me more about my eyes."

I couldn't help smiling. He was so adorable and sweet. He really was. But maybe race is too big of an issue. What am I saying? We're just sleeping together.

Pulling into a parking space close to Lystrom Hall I reached in the back for my backpack.

"You're really going to class?"

"Why wouldn't I?"

I heard a sigh as he leaned back in his seat.

"Are you really an honor's student?" I asked.

"Yes. I'm not getting a presidential scholarship or anything, but I make the Dean's list."

"Well, I did get the scholarship, so I need to go to class."

"Fine. Since it's paying for school you can go, but one of these days I'm going to get you to skip class."

"Highly unlikely."

When I opened my door, he reached over and yanked it closed. His hard body was pressed against mine and his face just a breath away.

"Tell me the truth. Wouldn't you rather come back to my room than listen to some boring old lecture?"

Yes. Yes please. Oh, hell, yes.

"It's a Monday. Don't make me have to remove you from the game for having too many fouls."

"I get two technicals, right?" he asked as his lips found mine catching me completely off guard. His tongue gently stroked my lips and I couldn't help myself and parted them. My hand, which should have behaved itself and pushed him away, instead chose to reach for his face. My fingers wrapped around his neck keeping him close and when he pulled back, I went for a second helping after I turned my head to the left for a different sensation.

"That was an intentional foul," I informed him when I finally felt strong enough to pull away from him. He was becoming a magnet to me. I couldn't help wanting to stay attached in what ever way I could.

"I don't think anyone saw," he whispered causing a light breath of air to tickle my lips because he hadn't chosen to move back, instead stayed tight to me.

"The ref did."

"It happened right in front of her. I had no chance of getting away with it. I think we should do an instant replay to make sure the home viewing audience knows about the infraction."

I licked my lips and turned my head to the side. "Why do you insist on pushing my rules?"

"I like staying after practice doing extra reps. Makes me stronger."

My heart pounded in my ears. He drove me crazy. I wasn't used to being pursued. To me sex was an exchange of time and a few fluids. The pleasure came from the adrenaline rush and the stimulation of nerves. But Tuck made it something else. He didn't seem to want to be detached from the experience as much as I had been used to. What scared me was he took me along for the ride.

"I think the muscle you're talking about is strong enough already."

CHAPTER EIGHT

W alking to dinner on Sunday nights was always a crapshoot of who would I see there. Usually nobody, but this night I didn't make it very far.

"Katie." A deep voice yelled causing me to slow down my pace. I turned to see Tuck jogging over toward me. "Katie."

"Yes."

"Where are you going?"

"To my ultimate doom. Dinner. I know it's senior-citizen time, but they don't serve after five on the weekends. Have you been on campus long?"

"I get that, but what I don't get is why you're not coming to the men's dorm."

"Because they only serve beer there?" I looked at him like he was insane.

"Can't you smell it?"

I breathed in deep to smell the wondrous odor of charcoal briquettes. My mind filled with the vision of the endless treasure trove of real meat and baked beans.

"I thought that was a neighboring house."

"No, it's us. You comin' to the barb-b-q?"

"I wasn't invited."

"I'm sorry." Tuck somehow dropped his voice another octave and stood at attention. "Ms. Katie Gills, your presence is requested at the McHenry dormitory for an old-fashioned Southern Barb-b-q complete with ribs." His voice returned to normal as he smiled at me. "Come on you'll be my guest." His elbow jutted out for me to curl my arm into it.

"I don't think I can."

"Is this one of the rules? Because I am asking my friend." He pointed to me. "You. To come to a social gathering that over half of the dorms will be at. Both male and female. We're celebrating since it was homecoming yesterday."

"Is that why there were so many old people at the game?" I teased.

"We won."

"I was there."

"You were?" He raised his eyebrow at me.

"You know damn well I was there."

"There was a cute girl sitting behind you. She's the one I winked at," he lied. "Come on, anything can happen at homecoming and I don't consider the weekend over until Monday at eight A.M."

"It still doesn't seem…"

"Is it because I'm black?"

"Why would you say that?"

"Cause now you're in a catch twenty-two. If you don't come, I can say it's because you're a racist who only talks to black people when others can't see. And if you do come then you break one of your rules. Which technically you're not breaking because you showing up at the same time as me does not constitute a date. You do not have to hang out with me for fear of public outing, or the fact that I rocked your world for the last four nights which by the way was also against the rules."

"How—oh weekend only. Right. I had a moment of weakness."

"Have another. Call your buddy…" He twirled his index finger.

"Mark?"

"Yes. Have him be there. I think salad-bar guy is there already."

"Thank you for that."

"So see all your friends might be there."

"I doubt it."

"How many friends do you have?"

"Rule breaker," I warned then started to walk toward the men's dorm. "I hate you, you know that right?"

"Kinda figured that out last night."

"Did you now?"

"Not only did you yell motherfucker over and over you looked mad at me for leaving. I would have stayed you know."

"I wasn't mad at you."

"Disappointed?"

"No." *Yes.* "You were following the rules for once."

"Gotta get my licks in between the whistles. Once they're blown, I have to behave. Coach taught me that." He smiled.

Laughing with Tuck and half of the defensive players while they were going back and forth smash talking each other I was able to be social. Sam crossed over to where I was sitting.

"Katie?" Her voice was light and airy setting me more on edge. Chance was standing right behind her following like a pathetic puppy.

"Hi, Sam."

"I need a favor." She sat down next to me and I could see the uneasy feeling Chance was having. "My boyfriend is coming to town Tuesday night."

"That's fun."

The guys kept talking, but I could feel Tuck lean his leg against mine. If I didn't know better, I'd think he was marking me as his.

"He wants to hangout, but I want Chance to be there too because I think they'd get along great. You know how it is when you have a guy as your best friend."

"I guess?" I could see the pain on Chance's face. It was almost as if I could see his stomach cramping up.

"We need a fourth so Chance isn't a third wheel. I'd hate to make him feel uncomfortable."

He's in love with you and you want him to go out with you and your boyfriend. Why would he ever feel uncomfortable? I don't know why Chance allows himself to go through this pain. He should step back and allow Sam to run her course with Dave.

"Mark never feels that way," I stated.

"You have a boyfriend?" She acted shocked by the idea.

"No. Not currently." Tuck's leg was pressing harder against mine, but he seemed to be pretending to be in the other conversation. I had the feeling he was ear hustling like a mother on my conversation.

"Trust me. Hanging out with two guys when one's your boyfriend is different. So would you be willing to be our fourth? We're going to see *The End Run* and get some pizza. My treat."

"That's not necessary."

Chance resembled a possum run over by a truck.

"I'll go. I wanted to see that movie anyway."

Tuck's leg disappeared from mine. I turned to see him getting up and grabbing more food.

"Great." Sam giggled and took off. Turning her head, she yelled back to me. "Six on Tuesday."

"Got it," I called after her.

Chance collapsed in the chair next to me. I placed my hand on his knee and leaned on his shoulder.

"Tell me I was not your idea."

"I wanted to stay home. I just can't say no to her. She thought of you because of all the help you've given me over the last year. You're adorable," he said sarcastically like a girl describing a *Hello Kitty* backpack. "Don't you know?"

"I'm sorry."

"She thinks I should try to date you."

"Is this a real date?"

"No. Yes." He ran his hand through his hair.

It's not like I hadn't thought about dating Chance. All the men in my rotation have the potential to be boyfriends. None have ever wanted to, if they did, I'd push them away. Chance gives me glimmers every once in a while he's thinking about it, but he's so hooked into Samantha I'd never wanted to be an afterthought.

"I know it's against the rules."

"No hand holding, or kiss goodnight and we should be good."

"What is it about her?" he asked like a man nearing death asking for forgiveness. "Ever since I've met her, I can't think straight. I never used to be like this. Do you know how painful…" I could feel him turn his head down to look at me. "Never mind."

Tuck returned to his spot and I lifted my head from Chance's shoulder.

"I'm not that coldhearted," I protested and heard a harrumph from Tuck. "You love her. It has to be painful."

"Any chance I could talk to you upstairs for a little bit?"

Now I was torn. Chance was really hurting, but Tuck was sitting right next to me and even though Chance was being quiet I could tell Tuck heard his request.

"That's not what you want right now," I consoled. "You and I both know that."

"I can't have what I want."

"When you're like this all you do is frustrate yourself."

He can't perform when she's got him twisted this bad. He knows that and so do I.

"I'm going to lay down," he said holding my hand in his as he stood up and pulled on it, but I didn't move.

"I'll check on you later."

"Okay. If you don't, I'll see you Tuesday. I'm so sorry, Katie."

"There are worse things in the world than free pizza and a movie."

He sulked into the dorm and Tuck spoke up.

"Why didn't you follow him?" he asked stabbing his plastic fork into some coleslaw.

"Tuck," I warned.

"He's in your rotation, isn't he?"

"The right to refusal is in the by-laws."

"Is it one sided?"

"Only when I'm by myself."

He stared at me and tried to figure out what I meant. When he got it he finally dropped the attitude.

"And you complain about me talking about sex."

I leaned over and whispered in his ear. "You would have said only when I'm remembering my hands gripping tightly to your hips as I ram myself over and over into you. If I choose to touch myself in a way to make me come so hard all I can do is scream your name to bring me peace I'm going down a very different path."

He laughed then looked at me. "Nah...I'd just say when I'm jacking off, waxing the skin boat, petting the lizard…"

Suddenly I noticed others were paying attention to us. A group who all decided to add their tried-and-true nicknames for self-pleasure.

"Spanking the monkey."

"Spit-shining the old water pump."

"Choking the chicken."

"Playing with my friend Charlie."

"Shaking hands with my best friend."

"Beating off." Mark joined in from the sidelines.

Everyone stopped and stared at him. Taking the focus off of Tuck and me even though he thought he was being cool. The whole bench burst out laughing.

"You gotta get out more," one of them joked.

They all started to pick with Mark and Tuck placed his hand on my knee. Scanning the area, he seemed to be under the impression no one was focused on us and slid his hand up my thigh then brushed his pinky finger in between my legs. Even though he wasn't touching bare skin he might as well have been for all the heat building from this light touch.

Leaning close he whispered right below my ear causing his breath to tickle my skin. "Come upstairs with me."

The hair on the back of my neck raised and a tingle went down my spine.

My eyes fluttered as my hand went to his squeezing it tightly.

"It's Sunday. Still the weekend. Come with me, Katie."

He had me in so many ways. I held back from showing him, but it took all my strength to not hop up with his every command and skip all the way to his room.

"I gotta go." Standing up I stretched then tossed my plate in the garbage can. Tuck looked down at his plate and shook his head. "Hey, Tuck, you done with my book?"

His head popped up then turned to the side. "I've gotten everything I need from it."

"Could I get it please? I think I'm going to head back to my room."

"No not yet," Mark whined. "You need to stay a little bit longer."

"I've got to study for the A and P test we have tomorrow."

"We do?" Then he got it. I was trying to head out. "I thought you knew Mittens inside and out? What am I saying, you want to know it blindfolded."

"That's how I plan to practice. Blindfolded."

"You going into urology?" he teased while I just shook my head.

Turning back to Tuck I knew I could leave now. "Book."

"Sure." He snagged his keys and we headed inside. His fingers swung on his side beside me brushing against mine. I could tell he was doing it deliberately.

By the time we made it to his room I was grabbing his hand and placing it on my waist. It's so large it wrapped around my whole hip.

"Is there something you're trying to say to me?" he joked throwing me on his bed. His lips found mine as I pulled on his shirt releasing his lips only for a moment so I could throw the garment off. The warmth of his skin soothed me. "I'm going to think you like me the way this is going."

"You said anything can happen at homecoming." I held tight to his body kissing his neck. His weight on top of me made me feel safe and secure. His hand slid down the side of my cheek grasping the back of my head. His tongue swept through my mouth massaging mine.

A fervor erupted between us turning me into an animal. I had one thing on my mind, and it was him. All the time Tuck. My hands clung to his biceps as his lips went for my neck then down my chest. A moan escaped my lungs as my back arched.

His hand slid across the small of my back and we rolled in his bed. Pulling back for a moment I opened my eyes to see him staring at me with delight. His finger wrapped around a loose hair tucking it behind my ear. My head turned into his hand kissing his palm. There was a look in his eyes telling me he wanted something, but I couldn't figure it out so I leaned down and kissed him again.

"Katie," he said as I started to pull off my shirt.

"Yes." I flipped the shirt off and tossed it across the room. Reaching behind me I started to unlatch my bra, but Tuck's hands held my hands against my back. Suddenly I felt trapped. "What's wrong?"

"Can we hang out?"

"Hang out? We were hanging out downstairs."

"You had your shirt on downstairs."

I scrunched my nose up and slid off his hips. He rolled over and set up on his arm.

"I wanted to touch you. Which I can't do in public."

"Are you—" I couldn't even say it. He can't be attaching. I'm not ready for this to be over.

"Maybe. No. Of course not. Can't I want to hold your hand? I'm respecting your rules, but there's more to you than your body."

"Since when?"

"Katie we've talked."

"After sex, yes."

"I'm out."

"Because I won't hold your hand?"

"Protection. Now I could walk down the hall and borrow some, but I'd get questioned."

Oh, that makes more sense. Hell, I think I'm out of condoms too.

"It's okay."

"Can I play with you?" He smiled and slid his hand over the top button of my pants.

"Play?" I smiled.

"Don't you ever play with someone other than yourself?"

"I don't play with myself. I was being silly out there."

"I'm not your priest so no reason to lie to me."

I dropped back on his bed ignoring his comment. What I couldn't ignore were his fingers that had released my right breast from the safety of my bra. This was followed by his lips which surrounded then sucked hard on my nipple, and finally his hand slid inside my pants.

I unbuttoned my pants allowing him to have full access. First one then two fingers glided inside me making my hips arch toward him as I moaned. His lips released and his tongue swirled around my nipple. All the while a wondrous rhythm had been created between my thighs. A third finger entered as his thumb started to rub on the outside of me. His lips were again on my neck as his tongue flicked against my skin.

I reached for his head to hold in place only to have him catch it with his free hand. He wrapped both my wrists in his large hand and held them above my head. I was trapped. I couldn't stop him from what he was doing. It thrilled me in a way I couldn't understand.

"I'm playing—not you," he explained while his tongue grazed my ear sending chills down my spine. His lips returned to mine as his rhythm increased. "Come for me, Katie."

"You don't own me."

His pace increased again as he twisted so slightly if it wasn't for the fact he must have actually found my g-spot I wouldn't notice, but it was the right spot at the right time and my whole body clenched as my blood pumped so fast I got light headed.

I love you! I screamed in my head. *Never leave.* His lips found mine again, but I could feel his smile knowing what he had done to me. Every part of me was alert and impassioned I would have promised him the world to keep going. But I didn't need to promise as he kept going and going before I knew what happened his head was between my thighs and I was pulling away because I was going to explode.

Sitting at the top of his bed I was panting trying to regain my composure.

"I don't think I can play with you."

"That's too bad because I think we're tied."

"Tied?"

"Overtime." His head dove between my thighs again as his hands locked on my hips. Sweeping his tongue from the top to bottom of my sex before entering the sensitive opening. Sucking lightly on the small button of nerves at my apex first, then more greedily until I came almost instantly still shaking from the last episode.

CHAPTER NINE

Leaving the cafeteria, I was laughing with Bryan and Gary.
"I forgot my bag. You guys go ahead I'll catch up."

"You sure?" Bryan asked.

"Yeah, I left it at the table."

"Okay," Gary replied.

After retrieving my bag, I walked back through the union and heard someone retching in the men's bathroom. The noises were pained and didn't sound like a hangover, but someone really sick. The sound of water running let me know the guy was going to be exiting soon. Slumped over I was able to make out a familiar form.

"Tuck? Are you okay?"

"No." His eyes drooped, and his body slumped.

"Cafeteria food?"

"I didn't even make it upstairs."

"Come with me," I ordered wrapping my arm around his.

"Huh?"

"You need someone to take care of you. Don't be a blockhead."

"I'll just go back to my room and crash."

"No, come on." I pulled him across campus and used my side key to get him to my room, just in case the dorm Nazi was working the desk. The last thing I needed was her demanding he leaves at curfew or worse yet reporting me to my RA. There was no way he could take care of himself.

In my room I dug through my medicine cabinet while he leaned against my dresser. Grabbing a new toothbrush, I passed it to him and smiled.

"Thanks." He crossed to my sink and started to brush his teeth while I pulled out the futon under my loft. After a few minutes he flopped onto the futon. I found the big quilt my grandmother made along with the fleece tie blanket from my high school team. I tucked him in and started to make him some *Thera-flu.*

"Sit up." I sat against my wall and had him lay between my legs with his head against my chest. Bringing my mug to his lips I blew on it from the side. "Drink."

"What is this?"

"Medicine."

"Drug tests."

"It's Tylenol and a sleep medicine."

"Then I need to go to my room. I know your rules."

"You're sleeping here. There's a difference between this sleeping over and that sleeping over. You have a fever and didn't walk straight on the way here. I'll take care of you."

"Why?"

"You're my friend. I take care of my friends. Now drink."

Finally, he took the medicine making me happy.

"That's bitter as shit."

"I never said the medicine tasted good. Here crackers cut the taste."

"You're trying to kill me."

"Maybe, but you're too weak to fight it. Drink fast and get it over with."

"Mean nurse."

"I know you prefer a naughty nurse, but today you get me."

He smiled, but he was too tired to fight with me. Drinking the liquid, he relaxed in my arms. "Okay, lie down. Are your muscles sore?"

"Ugh," was all he said. He started to tremble, and goosebumps covered his skin.

Pulling the blanket over both of us I began to massage his neck. It took everything in me to not kiss his exposed skin even though he was burning up. This was stupid I should just put him to bed and be done with him, but he looks so pathetic when he's sick.

Peeling off his shirt I worked my way down his back. Instantly I began to regret doing this, but he was already starting to drift off. So I allowed my hands to work finding the hardened muscles along his spine. Stretching out I realized I was laying completely on him and my lips were less than an inch from his back. I sat up and crawled out of the covers only to have a very large hand encircle my wrist.

"Don't go."

I didn't know what to say. He kept tugging me down on the bed and his arm wrapped around my waist.

"I'm going to get ready for bed."

"It's early."

"Well, I'm doing it because I'm just going to study and take care of you. Now go to sleep."

His head turned up and his eyes heavy with exhaustion looked at me. "Don't sleep in your loft."

"You want me to sleep with you?"

"I don't want you to get sick but—I want you to be close."

"If you let me go so I can get my stuff I'll sleep with you," I promised kissing his forehead.

"You're good people, Katie."

"No, I'm not."

The thoughts I was having for this patient would cause me to lose my license if I were a doctor.

Separate yourself, Katherine, your brother will be fine. Why do you coddle him? Her father's harsh words confused her. He was a doctor. A caregiver. One who had the ability to heal, but he stood over his own child without an ounce of sympathy. Instead he saw her brother as an annoyance because his temp spiked. The memory painful and had her wondering how her siblings and her weren't sociopaths.

Tuck's face was placid, and I focused on his breathing. It was deep and even letting me know his lungs weren't affected. If I saw him as a patient, I could control myself. A flash of the image of Mitten's body splayed out with pins stuck all over marking all her parts came into my brain and I gasped.

"Hmm. Huh." Tuck stirred so I grabbed my shower caddie, sandals and my PJs I shouldn't have any problem getting in the shower at six.

Walking down the hallway I entered the bathroom to see two other girls there. One was sitting on the counter the other giving her advice.

"Katie? Right?" I think the girl's name was Keyondra. She was dark as coal and had the most beautiful doe eyes I had ever seen. Her friend was what I had learned was called red boned. With a few traces of freckles, she tried to cover up and a red tint to her hair, but with all the dyes and colors in her hair it was hard to still see it. I only knew that from when she would walk around with product on her hair.

"Yes."

"You tutor a few guys, right?" Tutor, my rep was intact.

"Um a handful."

"Do you know a guy named Cedric?"

"Just in passing. He's friends with one of the guys I tutor."

"Is his friend Tuck?"

"Yes."

"You know Tuck?" Her eyes lit up at the prospect.

"It's only been a few weeks so as much as I can."

"Does he have a girl?"

She didn't see me as a threat. No one did. I was Katie the brain. No guy wants a brain.

"I'm pretty sure he does," I lied.

I'd never be a cock blocker for Chance or Kermit. Heck any guy I'd messed with. I never had a problem with them dating someone. Where did that come from?

"Back home or here?"

"Does it matter?"

"Yes. Because back home girls don't count," her friend pointed out.

Since when, was all I could think, but I wasn't one of those girls. The ones that hunted.

"What does Cedric have to do with it?"

"Cedric told me that one of his friends was interested in me, I'm pretty sure it was Tuck. I mean he's amazing looking, isn't he?"

Yes.

"I don't know."

"Don't sell yourself short." Now it was time for the advice giver to speak, only she was speaking to me. "If you let your hair down, put on some makeup and a short skirt I bet you'd think about how cute guys are."

Did she just call me ugly? I turned my head to see this girl with thick makeup covering fresh acne, some that had scarred. She was wearing coochie cutters and heels.

"Just not Tuck. You're right, Trinity. I'm going to call him."

"I don't know why you'd do that. Black men aren't worth shit."

My fist instantly clenched thinking Tuck was amazing. The protective nature I have for my friends in general tripled at the thought that this girl said he wasn't worth shit.

"He's getting his degree," Keyondra defended.

"I don't know why you believe that. He'll ride out his scholarship," scholarship was in air quotes. "Then leave. I bet he doesn't even take more than twelve hours. I'm telling you if you want a man that will take care of you, you need to look into the white guys that are curious then work that punanny magic on them."

I started my shower to get away from this discussion.

"Are you going to shower?" Trinity snapped.

"Yes," I replied thinking *no I wanted to come here and talk to you because it's so intellectually stimulating.*

"That is going to ruin my weave. All that steam and shit. We need to leave Keyondra. Fucking white girls thinking they can just do what they want when they want having no consideration for anybody but themselves."

WTF?

Keyondra poked her head back in. "Sorry, Katie. Could you ask Tuck if I was who Cedric was talking about? He never said who the guy was."

"I doubt it was Tuck, but I can ask him. I do know that LaDrell asked me if I knew you when I typed a paper for him once."

LaDrell never made it into my rotation, but it was because he wanted something serious. He was a good guy.

"LaDrell?"

"He runs track."

"Huh? Let me know about Tuck."

I should have expected that. If I had the choice of sleeping with Tuck's firm body and LaDrell's smooth sleek frame I'd choose Tuck every time too.

CHAPTER TEN

F inishing my shower, I walked back to my room to see Tuck shaking under the covers. His brow was now wet with perspiration, but he was still sleeping.

Snatching a hand towel, I started running water to make sure it wasn't too cool. I had never been one to use washcloths, but right now I was starting to regret that. Wringing it out I sat down and placed it on Tuck's forehead when he grabbed my legs and pulled his head onto my lap like a cat snuggling in for an ear rub.

Scooting back and keeping Tuck on my lap was an adventure. Luckily my books were beside me on the floor. I pulled up my Developmental Psych and decided to try to read until Tuck moved off me and I could work on Calc.

I readjusted the towel. His temp was starting to worry me. I went through all my checklists. Glands, heart rate, respirations, there I was breaking him down to determine the root cause of his current condition when he rolled over and stuck his face into my stomach. My fingers couldn't help themselves anymore. They traced the line that was cut into his hair. Not that he had much. I had seen him completely bald a few weeks ago so these were the first little prickles that appeared, but my hand still wanted to stroke his head like it was Chance's.

The tip of my finger followed the curve of his ear noting this was more round than oval. Down to his earlobe that had a medium sized diamond stud in it. Spinning it didn't seem to affect him. My finger traveled down his jaw, tracing his lips. His tongue came out licking his lips and catching my finger at the same time. I let my hand rest on his neck massaging lightly what I imagined was a tight muscle.

I went back to reading my book in the dim glow of my desk lamp with him holding tight to me. My concentration only broke when I felt him shiver or grasp me tighter, then I'd adjust his blanket to keep it over his shoulder.

After about an hour he started to grumble, and I could tell something was wrong.

"Tuck?"

He rolled over and I grabbed my wastepaper basket just in time for him to throw up again. He wasn't even fully awake. I went to the sink to get a cup of water for him and found him laying on his back on my bed.

"No, no, no. You're vomiting you can't lie on your back. You'll get aspiration pneumonia."

"What?" He gurgled and I rolled him to his side.

"Here." I passed him the water which he swished then spit into my trashcan. I'm glad my mom always made me use plastic bags in the there. "You done?"

"I don't think there's anything left."

Pulling out the bag I replaced it with one I had in the bottom and walked it down the hall to the trash shoot.

Back in the room Tuck was brushing his teeth and tried to smile when I walked in. I found my thermometer and placed it in his ear.

"I've never seen one of those outside of a clinic."

"Doctor's kid. We get all the perks."

"Good. Then I don't have to go to the ER."

"If I could write prescriptions, I'd say that was true."

"You think I need a prescription?"

"*Tamiflu* would be a Godsend right now. But a little TLC might get you through."

"How tender are you going to be?"

My hand stroked his forehead, traveled down his cheek then wrapped around his firm jaw pulling him close.

"102 fever and you can still proposition me. Impressive. No wonder all the girls want you."

"Who wants me?"

"Here's my dilemma. If I tell you then I may end up losing you in my rotation."

"That's a conundrum." There's that sexy brain again flexing in front of me. "I thought you weren't possessive."

"I'm not." *Except with you.* God, I don't want to share him. It was scaring me how much I wanted to lock myself away with him and never leave my room. Even sick I felt like this was what I wanted. Curled up in bed with him by my side for now and forever. *You're attaching so back off.* I dropped my hand and backed off.

"102?"

"Yep. I can give you ibuprofen to try to drop it. It's too soon for more Tylenol. This is going to sound ridiculous, but are you hungry?"

"There's nothing in my stomach."

"Okay, I'll make something, but we're going to teaspoon it to start with?"

I crossed my room, dug through my stash of food and found one can of chicken noodle. Cracking the top, I poured it into a bowl and started my microwave. Turning around Tuck had crawled back onto my futon and pulled the covers around himself again. He actually looked good for a guy with a high fever.

My dad had made me an emergency medical kit with everything he thought I'd need. The basics, but at the bottom was a samples box. A *Z-Pak* was tucked in there. I was given strict instructions to call him if I ever thought I needed to take any of these drugs. The supply was pretty good. I debated whether a *Z-Pak* was appropriate. I had no empirical evidence that this was a bacterial infection and his glands weren't swollen.

"What's that?"

"Medicine."

"That flu stuff?"

"Surprisingly no. I thought my dad gave me a little of everything. But *Tamiflu* is pretty new."

I tossed the *Z-Pak* back in the box and found the *Be-Kool* pads.

"This would be good?"

"That looks like it's for a five-year-old."

"What's your point?"

"Kicking a man when he's down."

"I cheat."

He smiled and I grabbed two of the patches. They pulled out fever, especially when it's viral and the fever reducers don't work. I stuck one on the back of his neck and one at the base of his spine then passed him his shirt.

"This should draw out your fever. I'd hate for you to get a chill."

The microwave beeped and I pulled out the soup. In my mini-fridge I had half of a blue sports drink left so I shook it in front of him.

"It's got my germs so if you want me to, I can run over to the union and buy you one. Our machines only have pop."

"I'm not afraid of your germs. You should be afraid of mine."

That's the one thing I never was. With how careful my father was I had never become the germaphobe I had seen his friend's kids turn into.

Passing Tuck the bottle and three Advil he smiled and swallowed quickly.

"Your throat doesn't hurt?"

"No."

"Headache?"

"Yes."

"That's probably the dehydration. I should have told you to sip that. Now you'll have to wait a few minutes before I can feed you."

"You're going to feed me?"

"Do you have a problem with that? I need to control your portions."

"That the only reason?"

"I told you. You're my friend."

Turning on the TV I sat beside him. Giving him a teaspoon of the soup at a time allowing thirty to sixty seconds in between each spoonful I made sure his stomach didn't reject it.

We spent the rest of the night with me changing out the *Be-Kool* pads and my wet hand towel. Medicating him when he was awake enough. He seemed to be able to sleep, but I was so nervous. Not about being caught with a man in my room more that I would do something wrong. His temperature finally broke around 6:00 a.m. I curled into his body as he held me tight, my mind able to sleep without running a million scenarios.

CHAPTER ELEVEN

Waking up alone on my futon was actually unsettling. The sun streamed through my window letting me know I'd slept the day away. Instinctively I reached for Tuck and found a notebook instead.

Didn't want to wake you. Thanks for last night I feel a million times better. Must have been all that great TLC. Good job, Doc.
   Your Friend Tuck

Below it was a drawing. He must have found my markers. It was like the ones little kids draw for their doctors. I was standing over him as he lay in the bed. All done in stick figures. There was even a little wastebasket by the bed. I crawled up in my loft and placed it at the head of the bed so every morning I could see it.

How goofy. I should just toss it. My fingers curled around the edges, but I couldn't pull it off. Smoothing out the paper my index finger traced Tuck's image laying under my loft.

Although I felt good now, I should wash my sheets and comforter. If I lay in those sheets, I could get sick. Jumping down I stripped the bed and retrieved my bottle of laundry detergent.

As I walked down the hall, I heard someone call my name.

"Katie Gills."

"Yes."

"You have an escort."

What am I? Someone who uses prostitutes? Well, in a way, I suppose.

I kept walking since I had to go by the lobby to get to the laundry room. Poking my head into the lobby I saw Tuck standing with his navy blue backpack.

"You here for me?"

He smiled and walked toward me. "I told you, girls come to me. Except one."

Following me down to the laundry room I had a smile on my face until I turned around and he could see me.

"Should I take this as an insult?"

"I'm sterilizing. It's nothing personal." Placing my basket on one washer I loaded the one in front of me. Tuck trapped me and started to kiss my neck. Shivers shot through my body causing my knees to go weak. "People could walk in."

"Sometimes I hate your rules." He backed off and jumped up on the table. "I feel a lot better."

"I saw the smiley face on your picture."

"You liked that?"

"It's my first good doctor picture. I'd frame it but—"

"People might know I'm your friend."

Placing the quarters in the slot I shoved hard to get the washer going.

"You're tutoring on a Saturday night?" Trinity poked her head into the laundry room.

"It's only four thirty," I said.

"Five hours before the night even really starts," Tuck added. "If I finish now, I can drink more and not have to worry about my hangover tomorrow."

"You did good today, Tuck." Trinity stated as she crossed over to Tuck and tried placing her hand on his shoulder. He leaned back.

"I don't like people touching me."

"I'm sure there's sometimes when you don't mind being touched." She leaned over on the table and I could see her cleavage being pushed up.

"You were supposed to play Lincoln today, weren't you?" I remembered.

"Yes, and what did you do while I was being pummeled?"

"Sleep. I was up all night with the flu."

"You were the one pummeling." Trinity hadn't realized Tuck and I we're in our own world that she wasn't a part of.

"That's too bad." Tuck winked at me. "Maybe you should have had a friend take care of you."

"I'll remember that next time."

"So, you'll be in Katie's room all evening?"

Tuck looked me in the eye and smiled. "Until I finish what I came here for." I held back my smile, but Tuck could tell he had me because he raised his eyebrow.

"Good I'll pick you up before we go out."

"Why?" he snapped setting Trinity back a few steps.

"I—I'm friends with Keyondra."

"Who's that?"

"Keyondra, dark skinned. Plays power forward for the basketball team."

"Never heard of her."

"We really need to get started on that paper," I said walking toward the door. Tuck hopped down and followed me.

"Who is that?"

"You don't know Trinity?"

"No. Should I?"

"I guess not." We turned the corner and hit the second floor. "Should I worry about my sheets?"

"If she trashes them, I'll get her back," Tuck assured.

"I think you may have already crushed her ego." My stomach grumbled embarrassing me. "That was rude. I'm sorry I missed your game."

"I wouldn't have made it at all if you hadn't cured me. How long did you sleep for?"

"Just woke up."

"Why were you so tired?"

I opened my door and tossed my basket across the floor. "Your fever didn't break until six."

"You stayed up all that time?"

"Yes."

"You're going to be a great doctor." His arms wrapped around me while he tackled me onto my futon. "Speaking of doctor."

"I'm hungry."

"So am I. You know what I want to eat?"

"I don't reciprocate."

"I made a run for the border."

My face flushed when I realized he might have not had a double meaning. "And now I'm embarrassed."

"Why? That's my dessert."

"Lay off the hot sauce then."

"I eat dessert first."

"Oh boy."

"I figured since I have a toothbrush here you wouldn't mind."

"Damn, you're a gentleman."

He slid down my chest and I knew he was serious. A trail of kisses were followed with pulls on my pants.

"Tuck?"

"Yeah, girl."

"I'm really hungry."

"So. Am. I." My pants flew across the room causing me to squeal. I never squeal. If nothing else I was having fun and enjoying his playful attitude too much. Letting myself go was not going to work.

"Tuck—"

"Is this one of those stupid rules of yours?"

"Kind of." I scooted up and away from him. "Let's watch a movie."

Which was worse? Allowing myself to hangout with him like a friend or letting him do something to me that was already exciting me, making every part of me tingle at the thought.

The paper bag poked out of his backpack and contained a soft taco and nachos for me. I crossed the room to get a pop from my fridge.

"You want?" I asked holding a pop up. Tuck was sitting with his arms crossed looking completely frustrated.

"I thought I made it clear what I wanted."

"You can leave if you like." I never was one to make any of my rotation hang out if I wasn't in the mood. What surprised me was how many still wanted to.

"I distinctly remember you being my dessert after the bar-b-que," he pointed out and heat seared a trail up my spine.

Had I? Damn him, he distracted me with an early orgasm breaking down my normal wall. Yes, occasionally I guess I slip, but today it felt wrong for some reason and it had been clearly established Tuck made me break too many stead fast, tried and true, rules.

His legs that were crossed at his ankles, started to rock.

"Is tonight not my night?"

"Excuse me?"

"Why can't I thank you?"

"That's why you wanted to do that?"

"Among other reasons."

"You brought me taco smell." The rhyming nickname always made me smile. "I'm good. I told you that I don't need payment for something I'd do for free." My pajama pants were at my feet so I picked them up.

"Put those on and I'll leave."

I turned to Tuck confused by his statement.

"I'm serious. It's bad enough you control what we do together I can at least enjoy the view in here."

Wearing boy short underwear wasn't sexy. What is wrong with this guy? And why shouldn't I control what we do? Who's the one with more to lose? Guys can only gain in popularity by scoring with girls.

"Fine." I took off my shirt too and threw it across the room. "Reciprocate."

"Reciprocate? I don't have a bra."

"Okay." I unlatched my bra and tossed that in the pile.

"The devil is your father, isn't he?"

"The theory's been put out there before. This is pretty frickin' cold."

"I was planning on you sitting by me."

"Touching? I can already see a problem with this," I replied eyeballing the stiff outline on his crotch.

"Haven't you ever just hung out with a guy?"

"Not naked."

"You're wearing panties."

"Now I can't eat." I crossed the room to grab my shirt only to have him catch me around my waist and pull me down to him. "Stop it. You're being a jerk."

"You're being a baby."

I pulled off his shirt and threw it over my head letting it fall around my neck as the smell of *Hugo Boss* came over me.

"Now I can eat," I stated plainly.

"Get me a soda."

"It'll cost you."

His fingers ran threw my hair as his lips found mine. Fused together I found myself caught up in a deep passionate kiss that overtook me and I didn't want to be in control tonight. As much as it scared me, I wanted him to control me. He pulled back and smiled at me.

"Get me my damn drink, woman."

He smacked me lightly on my ass. I jumped up and got him his drink. Bringing everything to my futon I curled my legs underneath me and rested my head on his shoulder.

He flipped on the TV and started scanning it as we ate. Every once in a while his fingers ran through my hair while the tip of his fingers trailed down my neck. Before I knew what happened we fell asleep. Breaking my ultimate rule. No sleep overs.

CHAPTER TWELVE

"Katie Gills…Katie Gills..."

I stretched and rolled seeing Tuck sleeping soundly next to me.

"Katie Gills."

Running out to the hall not remembering I was just in Tuck's t-shirt I pressed the button since the page was now going around the whole building. "Yes?"

"Phone call."

"Right—um send it—" I glanced down the hall to see which booth was open. "2546."

"Okay."

Stumbling I made it to the phone. "Hello."

"How many beers was it?"

"Kyle?"

"It is I. I'm driving through your little village on my way home. Any chance you'd have a few moments to spare for me or are you too busy curled up with someone."

"You know you're number one in my life. What day?"

"Tonight. I should be there around five. How 'bout dinner?"

"Love to. What time is it?"

"Noon my sleeping collegiate."

"Bite me, loser."

"That got me in trouble last time."

"Kyle, I can't wait to see you," I said with longing.

"Me too. Gotta run, Kitty Kat."

Returning to my room I was walking on air. I hadn't seen Kyle in almost a year. Tuck was starting to wake up and I had to kiss him.

"Good morning," he yawned and grabbed my ass. "Are you over being a drama queen?"

"Yes." I smiled, curling back into his chest. "I'm afraid to ask, but we missed brunch. Are you hungry?"

He kissed my neck. "A little."

"I have cereal and milk."

"Sounds good," he replied flipping on *NFL Sunday* coverage.

I held up two cereal boxes to which he scrunched his nose.

"Do you have anything that's not healthy?"

"Not really."

"I guess I'll go for *Cheerios* then."

I pulled out a couple of bowls and the milk and Tuck went into my bathroom. Hearing him relieve himself was a little unsettling. I guess I had never thought about that.

"Why is it?" he asked as he washed his hands, "that the girls get bathrooms and the guys don't?"

"I think they were an add on. I mean why would you have the sink in the room, but the toilet in what looks like a closet. It's only the single rooms that get one."

"Oh, well, at least I didn't have to wake you up to sneak me in the bathroom last night."

"You woke up and didn't leave?"

"Why would I leave? That's your rule not mine."

A knock at my door made me jump. I threw off Tuck's shirt hoping he'd put it back on as I grabbed a pair of jeans and a sweater.

"Who is it?"

"A random man wandering the halls endangering women."

I opened the door to see Mark smiling at me. "Who let you up?"

"Carrie's working the desk."

"And you wonder why I hate her."

Mark walked in and caught sight of Tuck then turned back to me. My face flushed as he laughed while crossing himself.

"So early and on the day of our Lord and Savior."

"You're the one dating the holy-roller. Don't take it out on me."

"You've already got your man stud stripped to the waist."

"Jealous."

"Yes. He never takes off his shirt for me, but with you he seems to never have it on."

"What do you want?"

"To save you from starvation, but it's probably not necessary."

He held a bag of donuts in front of me.

"Ohhhh," I said snatching at the bag.

He jerked it back. "Magic words?"

"I'll starve."

"Come on, it's one dinner. Bring Tuck if he owns a shirt. Oh, wait, he does I see. It isn't folded nicely, but looks strewn as if someone tossed it in some—"

"Stuff it."

"Lunch?"

"What does he want?" Tuck asked irritated by the conversation.

"Me to eat with his thing."

"That doesn't seem sanitary," Tuck stated.

I cocked my head to the side thinking how that would be—oh.

"No, his girlfriend."

"You'd like her if you got to know her," Kyle whined.

"No, I wouldn't."

"Fine then these are coming with me." He dangled the bag in front of me and I could smell the lemon Danish through the white paper bag.

"Cafeteria only. She can sit at my table. I'm not going to talk, and the others can interview her."

"Deal. I need to go. Carrie needs her nails painted."

"Does she keep your balls hanging over her bedpost or has she bronzed them like a trophy for all the world to see?" I asked.

"Gold plated around her neck so they're close to her heart."

"I'm so sorry I didn't realize you two were so special," I fawned and held my hands to my chest.

"Me either," Mark said glancing at Tuck.

"Don't assume shit."

"I've seen that look before."

"Then it's status quo."

"I don't think so." I shoved Mark hard into the hallway and turned back to Tuck. "Hey."

"You want me to go, don't you?" The tone in Tuck's voice carried an air of disappointment.

"After you eat. I think it would be best." I couldn't worry about his feelings right now.

A few hours later I had showered and was looking for something nice to wear. Not that I thought Kyle would take me anywhere fancy, probably a nice chain restaurant, but he tends to comment on anything I wear. Another knock on my door that could only be from Mark came around five.

"Are you naked?"

"Not yet. Come in."

Mark opened the door and smiled at me. "For me? You shouldn't have?"

I was standing in a pair of khakis and a black lace bra.

"Which is better, the blue or the purple?" I asked holding up two sweaters.

"I'm pretty sure that Tuck would like what you have on."

"I'm not going out with Tuck."

"Why not?" he asked flopping in my overstuffed chair. "You like him."

"He's a friend," I replied while holding up the light purple sweater under my chin and looking in the mirror.

"You haven't left this room in two days. How good of a friend is he?"

"He was sick. I took care of him. End of story."

"I heard sex cures everything."

"We didn't have sex," I snapped then realized we really didn't. We spent time watching movies and holding each other.

"Sounds like a relationship to me."

"Carrie still won't touch you, huh?"

"There are many reasons I don't want you to put on a shirt," Mark bemoaned. "Those are the only tits I've seen in months."

"If I let you touch them will you go away?"

"See, you're worse than her because you tease me."

"I know it's not fair. It's like putting a sex-a-holics meeting next to the free clinic. Nothing good will come of it." I pulled on the purple sweater and started to brush out my hair. "How tight is that chastity belt anyway."

"It goes up to her neck. I can't even cop a feel," he whined resting his head back.

"Is she worth the pain? I mean do you really want a virgin that bad? They're bad in bed because they don't know what they're doing."

"I beg to differ. I know one that knew what she was doing."

I threw my brush at his gut making him curl into a ball.

"Sorry. It was just an observation. I was hoping I could meet two unicorns in my life. Plus it's different for guys than girls. Katie if you get a virgin, you're liable to get stuck in your belly button or have some premature ejaculate but for a guy—"

"So the hole's a little tighter, making her more tense because we're programmed to think the first time is supposed to be wonderful and painful. You grin through it hoping it will end because the next time it'll feel good."

"I never thought about that?"

"What? That we're supposed to love and hate it at the same time? You guys wonder why we're neurotic."

"I never wonder with you." Mark was flipping a pen between his fingers. I had seen this a thousand times before. It always led to a stupid request. "Maybe you could talk to her about it not hurting. That's probably why she's so nervous."

"I'm waiting to see if that quarter between her knees turns into two dimes and a nickel."

"What do I need to say to her? This is why you're my best friend to tell me these things."

"I'm leaving you," I replied flippantly pulling the front part of my hair out of my eyes and securing it with a barrette.

"Katie," he warned drawing out my name.

With a sigh I went through the long list of bullshit men use with simple women. If nothing else Carrie was simple.

"I love you. Your eyes are beautiful. I'll never tell. I never buy a car without test driving it. Hi, my name is Mark. You say you love me but seem to be a sadomasochist that wants to see if the balls really do fall off. I don't know, ask for a hand job."

"She's afraid of semen."

"Excuse me?" I coughed. Thinking the delusional dimwit was going overboard now. This is why I didn't trust her. "Did you just say that she's afraid of semen? Is this a phobia? Smell? Taste? General color? Is there something you need to tell me about yours that's different?"

"The thought of semen makes her queasy."

"You told her there are different kinds of jobs, right. Hand verses blow? Tissue verses milkshake. What does she think will happen during sex to it? Or is she going to bring you close to climax then push you out of the bed so you can finish yourself off in private?"

"She said she thinks she'll be fine because it'll be inside her and she won't have to see it and that's okay."

"So after sex, that is in the five years from now when she gives it up, when she's sleeping you're going to somehow pull off the sheets and have them cleaned, pressed and the bed remade so she never knows about the wet spot, huh?"

"It's hopeless, isn't it?"

"Yes, honey. You want some, put in time with a person, not a robot."

"I heard that in the future there'll be robots that I can have sex with."

"Hopefully, they aren't afraid of semen. You want me to take off my shirt again?"

"No. My balls are already turning a beautiful shade of turquoise. When they hit navy blue are they dead?"

"Just like gangrene. You do realize it's not because she won't sleep with you that makes me hate her, right?"

"I know you think she's the devil."

"I've seen the mark. It's right above her left areola."

"That was mean."

"Maybe that's why you can't take off her shirt. Remember that dog like creature in the Omen. I think that's what's underneath her skin." Turning to the mirror I let the cherry Chapstick glide over my lips.

"Who are you going out with?" Mark whined.

"Avoidance."

"You should know. Who's worthy of lipstick?"

"It's Chapstick and you're deflecting."

"You're trying to sabotage the only guy you've ever liked."

"What are you talking about?"

"You like Tuck. So how 'bout you stop sleeping with him and start dating him."

"Who said we're sleeping together?"

"He's the only guy I've ever caught alone in your room."

"Aren't we alone in my room right now?" Holding my hands palm up, Mark scowled at me. "And aren't you still living out every cheesy teen movie playing the part of hapless virgin trying to get laid?"

"I never count as a guy in your life just like you don't count as a girl in mine. Plus you know I'm not a virgin."

"You're acting like one. That girl is leading you around by your nose. I mean seriously where is she now?"

"Studying."

"Without you?"

"I'm not in her science class, I'm in yours."

"Tragic."

"Again? Your date?"

"Katie Gills," the intercom announced.

"Appears he's here. You wanna meet him?"

"Yes. Any guy that gets you to put on girl clothes and war paint must be a winner."

I bounded down the steps and jumped into Kyle's arms as he spun me around. The traditional smell of Polo, the original, brought me back to all our times together. His brown hair always had natural blond highlights in with cool grey eyes and tough face that totally did not match his personality. The square head of a wrestler with a slightly crooked nose and the slight shadow of a beard trying to look unplanned, but I know him too well, it's the exact length he wants it to be.

My finger always instantly goes to his scar above his right eyebrow followed by a little kiss of apology. Of course he was perfectly put together. Looking at him you'd never think that he had been driving all day. Not a wrinkle on his straw-colored polo, black slacks or sports coat.

"Kitty Kat. How have you been?"

"Missing you but other than that fantastic."

"Hey, Mark, long time." Kyle reached his hand to Mark only to have Mark fall into his arms.

"You came to rescue me. I'm tired of being her gay best friend."

"Did you switch teams and not tell me?" Kyle laughed.

"Considering it."

"Katherine Alice, you need to go back upstairs and put on a skirt."

"Are those the pants that have only one leg hole?" I teased.

"Yes. You wouldn't have a dress somewhere up there would you?"

"No."

"But don't you have some sorority type formal to attend where post-pubescent males regurgitate on you?"

"No, and I'm not putting on a skirt. Look," I stated showing off my shoes. "Heels."

"Those are not heels. You will never correctly show off that ass in khakis and one-inch flats. Now go and properly dress for me. Mark, you have failed completely as a gay best friend. The only thing she got right was her eyes, but could those ever be wrong?"

"You win just because of the end of your rant. Fine." I stomped back upstairs to put on a skirt and heels, calling back as I stormed, "You're rubbin' my feet later when they hurt from those stupid ass shoes."

"Love you, Kitty Kat," Kyle yelled to me.

CHAPTER THIRTEEN

"So where are we going that required a skirt?"

"Oh, it didn't require a skirt. We're going to the Apple, but I figured you needed to feel like a girl."

"Applebee's. I'm wearing a skirt to Applebee's."

"Please, that's fine dining around here. Now spill. Who are you doing? And what are you learning about? Are they co-mingling? Playing doctor yet?"

"Actually, I did have a patient Friday, a traditional one, flu."

"Do I need to refresh you on how to play doctor?"

"I could use some pointers later, but now where are you at?"

Kyle filled me in on all that had happened in the few months since we last talked. The condo he bought making him a permanent resident and so grown up. He even got his own health insurance. I flipped through an envelope of pictures until we pulled into the parking lot.

Walking into the restaurant Kyle got whatever he wanted with the girls fawning over him as usual. The hostess sat us immediately and practically raped the poor man once we were seated. Somehow the last year in Atlanta had garnered him a great Southern accent, at least when he wanted to use it.

"Why are you going home?"

"Visiting some friends. I've got a meeting with an editor, remember my friend Charlene?"

"Redhead?"

"Yes. She's an assistant with an agency, thought I'd try to get a freebee from her."

"Money all gone?"

"You know I got the limited trust fund, not the real one."

A voice from behind me caught my attention.

"Seriously, man, where have you been all weekend? I didn't even think you'd make it to the game on Saturday. Covering for coach at curfew was hard as hell."

"I appreciate it." That was Tuck. "Trust me, I made it worth my while."

Oh, no, he didn't just out me. The pack of guys walked past us with Kyle's head turning to watch them pass.

"Why is your face red?"

"It's not."

"I know were both gorgeous but looking at me does not constitute a mirror, Kitty Kat." Now Kyle decided to work on his Southern drawl again. "Why you're redder than the Georgia clay, darlin'."

The group of players went around the bend and got seated in a booth that seemed to have a great view of me. This I realized when Tuck who was seated at the far end's face went from a huge smile to a glare and the whole booth turned to look. It was like the wave, first one guy then the next learning something interesting was on the other side of the restaurant. I heard some ohhhh snaps and Tuck's glare got deadly.

I don't know what I had done, but it was evident he wasn't happy with me. Swallowing hard I turned my attention back to Kyle.

"Katie, what's wrong?"

"Awkward situation. Now back to you. What's your book about?"

"Semi-autobiographical fiction."

"Oh, please say I was only spoken of with kindness."

"Mostly," he joked as he stroked his eyebrow with the scar.

Our appetizers came and I tried not to look at Tuck, but the glare was not going away. That's it I had to confront him.

"Excuse me, Kyle."

"Sure, do you want a refill?" He pointed to my pop.

"Thanks." Crossing the restaurant, I went straight to Tuck's booth. "Can we talk?"

Now Tuck decides to lean back and play it cool. "Me? Do I know you? Why would you need to talk to me?"

"Really? We're going to play that?"

"Play what? I'm not playing shit. You're the one that seems to be playing."

"So we're going to do this in front of the team?"

He looked left then across the table to his friends that were all being quiet, but their eyes were judgmental as hell.

"I'll be back."

"Yeah, sure man, handle this."

"Handle what?" I snapped. Tuck grabbed my upper arm and pushed me to the corner. "What are you going to handle?"

"That you are disrespecting the fuck out of me."

"How?"

"Because you're my girl."

"When did that happen? You said you wanted one thing from me nothing more."

"How many guys are getting that one thing?"

"Fuck you." I shoved him, but that was useless. His muscular chest and stance might as well be set in cement.

"How about we fuck your rules? I want to know."

"I need to get back to my date. You know, dinner, conversation maybe a movie not just coming over to fuck me then leave."

"Are you going to sleep with him?"

"What is wrong with you? You can sleep with whoever you want, but I can't even go out with a guy."

"Who? Who am I sleeping with?"

"I don't know, but you said—"

"You're the only one I'm with. Have been since our first night."

"Then why did you say that it was just sex?"

"Because that night it was."

I shook my head. He was serious.

"You gotta call an audible when you change a play. There hasn't been any change in how we act around each other so why would I think you wanted to be exclusive?"

"The commitment phob? You freak out—Don't you—want to—"

"Be with just you?"

Only since the first day. The thought still terrified me. But I had just been with him this last month or so. Sam's double date aside I was with him. If I did this I could get hurt. I would no longer be in control; it would all be on him. How could I protect myself? Tuck's eyes stared into mine and I knew it was time to take a chance. I think.

"Yes. Maybe. Yes."

"Why maybe?"

"Because it scares the shit out of me."

There's a difference between blunt and straight forwardness and all out honesty. Showing my weakness. Admitting my flaws. Standing three steps away from the damn bathroom in an Applebee's I might as well be naked before Tuck and letting him see every inch of me. Had I exposed too much?

"I promise, I won't hurt you," he pledged stroking my cheek with the back of his hand. My head turned into the caress of its own accord I was already starting to lose myself in him. "Why are you on a date?"

"Because I deserve one."

I stamped my foot and clenched my fists more to stop the flood of emotions running through me. The elation was more than I could handle.

"Have you been seeing him long?"

"First date."

"How's it going to end?"

"Tell me—truthfully—you want there to be an us? Holding hands in public. Making goo-goo eyes. Sharing feelings, hopes, dreams aspirations, all that bullshit."

"Not the eyes thing."

"Then I guess we'll have to rock paper scissor to see whose room we're staying in tonight, because these last few days—" The sexual tension highs and lows broke through me.

"Don't go back to the table."

"Did you drive?"

"No, but we can fit you in Cedric's car."

"Nope, I'm going to finish my meal and you can meet me at the dorm." I started to walk past him only to have him grab me around my waist leaning down to my ear.

"You want me to fight him for you?"

"Tempting, but no."

"He doesn't look happy."

"That's because I've been gone too long."

"Has there been anybody else?" His voice was low and gravelly in my ear.

The strong possessive nature was overcoming me, and I could feel the gooseflesh tingling on my neck.

"No. I've been out of rotation, but I do like that you're jealous."

"I'm not jealous."

"Then when I go back to the table, I'm going to give him a good long kiss."

"Try it," he growled. "See what happens."

"Fine, come here."

Intertwining his hand in mine I pulled him past the table of players. A dozen eyes burned into me as we passed. Tuck's hesitation made me have to yank his arm.

"Come on," I barked testing to see how much I was his. If he followed with his boys watching I knew he meant it.

"Yeah, Tuck, you better go, massa calling," one of the guys called.

"Why you all up in my Kool-Aid when you don't know the flavor?" Tuck called back.

"Oh, we know the flavor," one of them snapped. "And it ain't black cherry."

"Are you coming or not?" He glanced at me then at his friends.

"I'll be right back, gotta handle my business."

"All right then. Handle your business, don't let your business handle you."

Walking toward my table I shook my head. "You really need to get over yourself."

"What am I supposed to say?" he asked. "Those are my boys."

"And?"

"And what?"

"Never mind."

"I can't let them know you have me whipped."

That stopped me in my tracks. I'd never whipped anyone before.

"You're whipped?" I asked and lifted my brow.

"You don't look like a girl that's good in bed. You walk wrong, you sit wrong, but girl…" A low whistle told me I had rocked his world. WTF? "The things you do—I understand why the other guys stayed quiet. I would do anything to keep you."

Sitting down I smiled at Kyle. His head instantly turned to Tuck standing above us.

"Hello?" he said.

"This is Augustus Tuckman. You can call him Tuck," I introduced.

"Nice to meet you, Tuck." The confusion on Kyle's face was comical as he extended his hand to shake Tuck's.

"Uh huh." Tuck's hand reached for Kyle's. "I'm her man."

"Good to know," Kyle tilted his head to the side and quirked his lips. I had to laugh.

"Tuck, this is Kyle. Kyle Gills, my brother."

Tuck pulled back his hand as his face went from 'I'm-going-to-murder-you' to gentleman in two point three seconds.

"Your brother?"

"Yes, he's passing through on his way to Chicago so he thought that he should feed his starving college student of a sister. Truthfully it is the first time he's taken me out."

"On a date…" Tuck's tone was amazing. I loved when he got that low grumble deep in his throat.

"We're on a date now?" Kyle asked.

"Someone was being a brat." I giggled.

"Was it me?" Kyle queried. "Did you want to have me killed? Seriously, was I that bad of a brother?"

"It was me." Tuck fell on his sword as he sat down next to me. "I wasn't treating your sister the way she deserves to be treated."

I could feel my whole body heat up. Sliding my hand on Tuck's leg gave me an anchor to steady my nerves.

"Is this your flu patient?"

"Yes."

"Pity to waste that body on medicine alone. Let me warn you about the Kitty Kat. She's spoiled, rotten and the biggest whiner you'll ever meet."

"So what you're saying is—"

"Run while you have a chance."

"Hey, now." I scrunched my face in frustration.

"I was going to say perfect." Tuck came to my rescue.

"I'm under legal obligation as her big brother to tell you if you break her heart—sorry sis—pick someone smaller and I can kick his ass. What happened to the lightweight wrestlers you liked?"

"When did you ever kick a guy's ass for breaking my heart?" I questioned.

"I thought about it once." Kyle took a sip of his drink.

"Once. You had a thought once."

"When did a guy break your heart?" Kyle questioned. "Usually I was stuck consoling them."

"But you liked that."

"Am I missing something?" Tuck asked, but Kyle and I were in the middle of our tête-à-tête.

"That's why I liked the little wrestlers," Kyle teased. "What did you tell me? They were small, compact and easy to ride?"

"My brother has chosen an alternative lifestyle," I said trying to catch Tuck up on the conversation.

"And I thank you for picking up the big black man so I don't have to be the black sheep of the family anymore."

"Really? You think me dating Tuck is worse than you dating Lance."

"We'll see at Thanksgiving. By the way I'm here for you when she breaks your heart."

Tuck got nervous and turned at me. "I don't think that will be necessary."

"That's what they all said." Kyle let out a little sigh.

Our waitress passed by and Kyle's hand reached for her.

"Sorry about the inconvenience. Our friend here is going to be dining with us. Could his order be brought to our table?" Kyle was back on Georgia speak.

"I'm sure I could do that," the waitress replied with a smile and nod.

"Could you bring us another order of these fine wings too?"

She blushed and leaned in. "I'll be sure to rush those just for you."

"Much obliged."

She walked away and I had to laugh.

"Kitty Kat, just because I don't like the pussy doesn't mean I can't use its owner to get me a saucer of milk."

"Okay, one, you've been in the South way too damn long. And two, don't talk about pussy after you call me Kitty Kat. It's a little creepy especially with that accent. You're from Chi town please talk like a normal person."

"For you anything." Kyle went back to his normal voice and turned to Tuck. "I told you she's spoiled. Tell me everything about your deep romance."

I rolled my eyes and leaned on Tuck's shoulder. His arm wrapped around my waist and we spent the rest of the night talking.

Before we moved on to dessert the team walked by and picked with Tuck for leaving them high and dry. Kyle smoothed it over like he smoothed everything over. The Kool-Aid guy kept glaring at me making me feel uncomfortable. It was then I thought about what he had said. *It ain't black cherry.* It was in that moment I realized it wasn't just the girls that had a problem with mixing.

CHAPTER FOURTEEN

"Are you dating me to piss off your family?" Tuck's finger was running along my leg while his lips seem to find the perfect bend in my knee.

He won the rock, paper, scissor game so we were in his room. I liked his better since he had put two twin mattresses together to make a king size bed. But he only had a sink in his room, and I wasn't going downstairs to use the bathroom so he always had to guard the door to the men's room.

"Why would you think that?"

"Your brother. If you are that's fine, I just need to know where I stand with you."

"Are you dating me because white girls give the best head?"

"They do? Would you care to demonstrate? I mean how can I make a fair assessment if I've never received the services? At least not from you."

"Stereotype. Little white girls with daddy issues. Don't stereotype me."

"Your brother brought it up," he pointed out.

"To get me and you to fight. That and he's been pissed off since Lance."

"Who's Lance?"

"My father's fishing buddy. Dad caught them together and let's just say Lance wasn't pitchin'.'"

"What does that have to do with what your brother said about you being the black sheep now?"

"I like you, isn't that all that matters? Plus getting attention in my family was never my strong suit. And why would it be okay for me to be using you like that?"

"I'd get a lot more sex with no strings."

Grabbing a pillow I smashed him in the face knocking him back so I could straddle his hips. "You said you wanted strings so you better take that back! Take it back now or I'll—"

"You'll what?" he asked grabbing hold of my ass and pushing the stupid skirt up turning it into a belt.

"I can't think of anything you wouldn't enjoy," I said with a wink.

"Speaking of which I heard white girls are great at giving head."

"Not gonna happen."

"Please."

"You haven't earned it."

"What do I have to do?"

"I don't know," I replied. "Nobody's earned it with me."

"Really. How about I go back and beat up all the guys that broke your heart for you?"

"How about you drop it?"

"Oh, come on, please. Some stereotypes are true. Look at me. I'm black, I'm a man, I think there's a stereotype of mine that you like." He squeezed my ass tight and I leaned in to kiss him.

"That you have big feet?"

"Exactly."

"Stereotypes are not true. There are some black men with tiny feet."

"How would you know?"

"Oh, I'm sorry, did you think you were the first?" I straightened my back.

"Guy, no. But black guy most definitely."

"Why?"

"You haven't gone through the black by injection reaction."

"Now you know why I insist on protection," I joked. "Look, I know I don't talk ghetto, wear baggie clothes or use the n word—"

"Did you just say n word?" He laughed at me. "Say it. Call me your—" I kissed him. I hated that word, always had, always would. Just the way his lips formed when he said it was disgusting like watching a five-year-old say fuck or shit.

"You're mine."

He looked at me as the light from the lamp lit up his dark brown eyes. "I'm yours."

"And I'm yours."

"I never had me a little white girl."

"I'm gonna kick your ass in a second."

"You're right, all your punishments sound so fun." He flipped me over so he was on top. My legs locked around his waist. Tuck was hard as steel and he teased me by rocking his hips.

"Can we try something?"

"What's that?"

"Really be with each other."

"Like deep passionate love making?" he joked.

"I don't know about passionate. We've been having fun, but I've been afraid to let myself go."

"You're not going to get all freaky on me and start listing weird sexual things? If so, I need to stretch."

"No. I didn't want to get hurt so I haven't been all there. Do you know what I mean?"

"I always bring my A game."

"Can we be serious for a second? Or was my sarcasm the turn on?"

Tuck's voice became solemn and his hand stroked back my hair as he leaned in close. "Your eyes were the turn on. Followed by your lips that seemed to always say the right thing. But do you know when I fell in love with you?"

Did he just say love?

"I don't think I've ever had anyone take care of me like you did. It wasn't coming from some sense of he's a star or he can get me something. You were genuinely concerned about me as a human being. Do I want to make love to you? Most assuredly. Am I scared to death of it? Petrified. Because I'm already sprung on you so bad it hurts to be apart from you, but I can't let anyone see that."

"Show me. Show me how it hurts."

His fingers ran under my hair as he leaned in and our foreheads touched. He was shaking as he slowly came to my lips. I could feel the heat building between my legs, but I didn't want to rush because the sensation was new to me. I was afraid of what was happening. Unsure of if I could do it. I asked for it, but he gave in too easily.

Was this what it was like to have a guy sprung on you? His free hand had been on my knee and crept its way up my thigh. Finally, releasing my lips, he found my neck. His hand, that I was so sure was going to stop at my hip, kept moving up causing goosebumps as it passed my ribs.

The shirt I wore moved by his hand and I extended my arms so he could remove it. When the garment was over my head, I opened my eyes to see his smiling at me. Finding my lips again his hand kept working up my arm until our hands were intertwined. When he gazed down at me, I panicked.

I had never done this before. Not sex with meaning. My heart started to pound out of my chest as my head swam. The one time I thought I had the other person wasn't there. This would be both of us there at the same time, with the same feelings. Maybe I'm wrong. Maybe he's Clark all over again.

"Stop."

"What's wrong?" he asked.

"I can't do this. I'm not ready."

"Ready for what?"

"This. I don't know how to do this?" I pulled back and tried to push against his chest.

"I beg to differ. You're actually very good at it."

"Not like this. With—with—"

"Meaning."

"I don't know how to not block or receive."

"Katherine." Tuck's eyes were on mine. "I love you so please show me you feel the same."

My heart pounded from fear, skipped, and I found his lips again. Could I really let go? The smoothness of his skin against mine was lulling me into a soft space. While his cologne sent a warm wash through my system.

"You said you trust me," he whispered.

I did? I can't believe it, but I did.

"Are we good?"

"We're good."

Entering me it wasn't like it had been before. Nerve endings finding a way to be stimulated for the expected response. You hit the patellar tendon you will get a knee jerk reaction. You rub two parts together you should get a reaction. But this wasn't the natural nerve stimulation. We weren't just two bodies rubbing together, we were one being working in unison. I was actually one with someone.

Fear and pleasure were working in concert as I tried to pull back. Tuck held me tight as if he could actually feel the subconscious action inside of me.

"Not this time," he ordered as his tongue tickled my collarbone. "I'm yours, take me."

We rolled in the bed letting me be the lead. He was letting me get what I wanted from the experience. Holding back when I told him not yet. Faster, harder, slower, softer, hands here or there. Whatever my request he filled it. Never before had I truly gotten what I wanted from a sexual experience. Touching what I wanted touched going when the sensation felt good, better, OMG.

When I thought I couldn't take anymore he gave it. My body lay shaking as he kissed me from the top of my hip up my spine until he found my ear.

"You love me," he whispered.

"I love you." Holy shit I meant it. My arm curled around so I could hold tight to his head. "Please don't hurt me."

"Never." His hand held tight across my stomach. "You are so fucking hot."

"The aura of sexual gratification."

"Shut up. I've always thought that. Every guy wants you."

"Whatever."

"Katie, do you not see how sexy you are? That and the fact that every guy thinks you're untouchable."

"Until you had to run your mouth and say you had me."

"Hell, yeah."

"Have you noticed no one else has said shit about me."

"Because they don't love you," he said.

"So guys only brag about their conquests when they like the girl."

"No. Usually they don't say anything unless they want to keep guys away, they do."

"So you were peeing on me."

"In a manner of speaking. I wanted the rotation to end."

"Asking me was too hard?"

"I wasn't the only one who was pretty clear about how they wanted this to go."

Rolling over I faced him, but he still kept me close as my foot glided up his leg then hitched around it so I could lock myself on him.

"You scare me to death."

"I don't know who hurt you, but I could never do that." His fingers lightly stroked back my hair as he leaned into my ear. "Katherine Gills, I love you, I'm yours and will be forever. You're not the only one scared. I've never felt about anyone the way I feel for you."

I was somebody's and he was mine.

CHAPTER FIFTEEN

Entering the lobby for the cafeteria the fear of Clark came back to me. The promises of everything only to have him hurt me more than I ever thought possible. My fingers slid into the small pocket of my backpack and retrieved a swizzle stick. Twisting and untwisting the plastic around my finger as each footfall up the spiral staircase added five pounds to my feet.

Tuck was bringing me back there as I hit the top stair, where I could see three girls around him. He was sitting on the couch, Keyondra was on the chair next to him, Trinity was seated right beside him and Shawnda was behind him leaning down. All were laughing at something.

My first inclination was to turn tail and head back to my dorm room. Anything to not be around when he ignored me. My hand twitched, sweat beaded down my back and I'm sure my top lip had completely disappeared because I bit it so hard.

"You okay?" Mark asked as I shook my head no.

Why did he have to lie to me? He was getting the sex. Why did he need to have me feel something more? Worst of all why did he tell me he loved me?

"Katie," he yelled, and I realized my hand was holding so tight to the top of the railing it cut into my hand. "Baby girl, come here."

Baby girl? His hand motioned to me and I saw the evil glares from his entourage. He wasn't moving on, if anything he was announcing I was his and he was mine. I caught sight of Chance standing in line suddenly becoming interested. Guess it was now or never. I also guess I can't just do my normal thing. I'd need to step it up. He wasn't some simple guy calling for me to help him with his history report. He'd asked for his Baby Girl to come over.

Releasing the banister I walked with about as much assuredness as a newborn cub learning how to tackle their prey. I could see the lionesses looking at me to see if I had what it took or if I'd just be a side dish they devoured for looking at their gazelle. Tuck's smile let me know he wasn't looking for me to walk over and say hi. He wanted to mark me as much as I wanted to mark him. At least I hope so.

With less than a step to go he hadn't moved from his spot and neither had the girls. It's not that I didn't have other options, I just didn't want to do them. We were both dropping our rotations. Publically. My legs straddled him like I had been for the last month as his head leaned back and I kissed him like he'd been gone for a year not just a few hours.

His hands were firmly holding onto my ass as I licked his lips and fell into a place where inhibitions disappeared as well as the rest of the world. When I pulled back, he smiled at me.

"Did you just pee on me?" he asked as my face flushed.

"Am I that wet?" I asked thinking no man's that good of a kisser.

"I meant you marked me."

"Oh. Well you're mine in case you forgot."

"I didn't forget. I just didn't think you'd have the nerve."

Sliding to the side of his lap he took my hand in his and slowly unwound the swizzle stick around my index finger. Blood pumped into the darkened digit letting me know my pulse.

"You really need these still?" he questioned placing the misshapen straw on the armrest for his chair.

"Probably, at least a gross of them."

"Fine, but you need to make me one with a football helmet."

CHAPTER SIXTEEN

"I'm going to have you screaming my name."

"Doubt it."

"Come on, you say fuck a lot just switch it up." Tuck had me pinned to the bed after we'd gotten back from starting a load of laundry.

"I do not."

"You do to. I'd have thought you more religious screaming oh my God, oh my God. Which of course would be another easy thing for you to substitute my name for, but you must be part sailor."

"You want me to say. Tuck me, Tuck me, Tuck me. Oh, Tuck me harder." I leaned back and did my best Meg Ryan. "Oh, Tuck me, Tuck me. Oh, Tuck."

"The last one was good. What scares me is your script sounds too familiar. Don't tell me you've been faking it. Oh, screw it, lets get out the video camera you're ready for your close up."

Ice ran through my veins. Video clips with hard grains around the edges flashed through my mind. The sound of cat-calls echoed from painful memories. Shoving Tuck off me I snapped. "Leave. Leave now."

"Katie, I was joking around."

"Leave." Tears stung the corners of my eyes and fire burned in my throat. "Leave."

"What did I do?"

I climbed up into my loft and curled into the fetal position. He could stay there all night for all I cared, I wasn't moving. Fear and shame were taking over me.

"Katie, you're nineteen-years-old so quit acting like a child." He shook the loft. "You know if I come up there your loft will collapse. You seriously aren't going to say anything."

Shaking from rage started and I kept my eyes closed tight.

"Fine, I'll leave. I don't like playing games."

A whimper escaped and I bit my lip. No one sees my weak side and now Tuck's seen two of my biggest weaknesses. He keeps finding the vulnerable parts of me.

"Katie, just talk to me. What did I do wrong? I thought we were just messing with each other."

I wiped the tears away and sat up with my back to him. "No one, but Mark knows." My voice was raspy, and the words had to push past the razors in my throat. "Do you set out to find all my issues?"

"I just want to know what I did, then I'll leave."

"Please, don't, I shouldn't punish you for someone else's behavior."

"Katie, I don't roll like this."

"Fine. Then go. You're right. There is no us."

"You just gonna toss me like that."

In my mind I was yelling no. Saying the reality was not what my imagination was showing me. I knew I needed to stop him. I had already given him one chance by making him my man. Breaking every rule in my book. At least every rule I planned on having until I was at least thirty-five.

I heard my door close and laid back down. My head pounded as the memory of that day haunted me.

· · ·

In the tenth grade I was in love with Clark. He was adorable. My ideal boyfriend who had totally pulled me in within two weeks. He was short with a nice tight compact body. His hair was longer in the grunge look split down the middle. With a guitar, tight pants and kisses that tasted like Juicyfruit.

Somehow, he had talked me into losing my virginity to him Telling me he loved me and would be with me forever. The stupidity of ignorance. I didn't know what I was doing so I listened to what he said. Following what he wanted.

The next day I met him at his locker still floating on the love coursing through me only to have him glare at me like I was crazy when I tried to kiss him.

"What do you want?"

"What are you talking about?" I asked reaching for his hand only to have him pull away. "Clark, honey."

"Stalk much."

Confused, I stood there crushed. Then he wrapped his arm around Tiffany Snyder's waist, and they walked to homeroom together as if I didn't even exist.

My world crashed around me as I ran to the girl's room to cry. Coming out for first period I saw a few guys snickering at me, but I kept walking. Mark came from behind and pulled me out of the school. Before I knew what was going on, we were ditching.

"Mark, you know my dad will shit if I don't go to class."

"You slept with Clark."

"How did you know?"

"Because he taped it."

"What?"

"Yes, he set up a screening for the guys that did weight-lifting this morning."

"He doesn't lift weights. You're lying."

"Am I really?" He pulled out a VHS tape with my name on it. "I

got it from him, but he just laughed at me and said it was a copy. So I say we break into his house and get the original."

"Why would he do this?" My throat tightened.

"Because he's an asshole, but you wouldn't believe me. Jesus, Katie, how long have you been with him a day and a half?"

"No. It was longer. He said he loved me."

"What have I told you a thousand times?" Mark's voice was strained.

"You're the only one who really loves me, and guys will say anything to sleep with me. But why? I'm nothing special."

"Not anymore." A dagger shot through my heart. "I didn't mean it that way. You lost the virgin status now you're moving on to the easy prey status. Come on which room is his bedroom?"

I looked up at Clark's brownstone and started to walk back to school.

"Katie—Katie—"

"Forget about it. My mistake, my consequence."

"Do you know what I had to go through to get this copy away from him? I had a room full of pumped up jocks."

"Did they try to beat you up?" I asked.

"They grumbled and called me a kill joy."

"What were you even doing in the locker room?"

Mark flexed his arm making me laugh for the first time. "Look here, Olive Oyl, I'll be Popeye someday. Why aren't you more upset?"

"You know I'm upset. You also know—"

"That on the outside you're cold as ice."

"Yes."

Mark held me tight. "But only on the outside."

He really was the only one who knew who I really was. If only we were attracted to each other I'd never have to be hurt again. Neither of us wanted to force a relationship, because we both knew it wouldn't be fair to either of us and we didn't want to lose what we had.

"Are you really going back to school?"

"Why wouldn't I?"

"I don't know because the guy you're in love with turned out to be an asshole."

"You mean the mistake I made people actually caught instead of just me. Minor detail."

"What about the original?"

"I'll get it from him. If I steal it, he'll know he hurt me."

Calming myself I snagged my quarters and headed down to the laundry room. As I got downstairs, I heard male voices coming from the laundry room over the light hum of the dryer.

"Look I don't know what she did to get it back, but she was in her room crying for three days. She'd come out when expected and went to school like everything was normal but inside—"

"She was destroyed."

"You better mean what you said about how you feel for her. I've never told that story to anyone."

"Did she start the rules in high school?"

"I don't know anything about her rules, but she never had a boyfriend after Clark."

"Traitor," I barked coming into the room ready to kill. "How much did you tell him? Did you keep one of the videos you sick pervert?"

"Katie Gills, you know better than that."

"How are you still here?" I snapped at Tuck. "Where's your escort because it sure as hell isn't me."

"I was here to see my lady—" Mark started.

"Bitch. Traitorous bitch."

"It really still hurts this much," Tuck interjected.

"You—you need to leave. I'm tired of you and your—" I couldn't get it out. I crossed to my washer only to see it was empty. "That bitch fucking cunt whore. I'm going to kill her." I turned around only to hit the wall again. I tried to move, but Tuck had me surrounded on all sides.

"The other guys never got to see this beautiful side of you, did they?"

"Leave me alone. I need to get my clothes."

"They're in the dryer. It was the least I could do." Tuck stayed calm making me even madder. The fact I couldn't control myself was so infuriating I could just spit. "Now I feel honored."

"Shut up and let me go."

"No."

"Let me go."

"No."

"Mark."

"I'm staying out of it."

"Now you're staying out of it. After you put everything out there."

"Oh, come on, Katie, you know I'd never—"

"Betray my trust. Well you have. Now go away I'm embarrassed enough already."

"Why? Because we both know you're human?" Mark quipped.

"Screw you."

"Does she get violent when she's angry?" Tuck asked.

"I don't know." Mark shrugged. "I told you I have no idea what she did to Clark."

"Did he walk funny at school the next day?"

"I'm so happy my humiliation has brought you so much entertainment," I snapped. "What else did you tell him?"

"There's more?" Tuck asked then held his hands up in surrender.

The dryer buzzed and I pulled out my clothes.

"Mark, are you done yet?" Carrie had arrived with her tight curly blond hair bouncing and her nasally voice two octaves below a dog whistle grating on my nerves.

I ran my fingers through my hair hoping to get that shrill noise to escape my brain.

"Yes, honey."

"Yes, honey," I mocked under my breath and Tuck smirked at me as he helped with my clothes on the folding table.

"Hi, Katie, feeling better?"

"She knows too."

"That you had the flu?" she replied. "Tuck was asking Mark about what to do to help you. Why I couldn't be here I'll never know?"

"Come on. I need to nurse a beer in your room," Mark replied escorting her out of the line of fire.

"God, she's sooooo stupid." The immature strain in my voice triggered Tuck.

"Are you jealous?"

"Of what? The fact that if she didn't wear those big clumpy shoes she'd probably float away like a hot air balloon."

"Are you in love with Mark?"

"God, no."

"You both say the same thing. Why is that?'

"Because we're best friends."

"Seventh grade?"

"Seventh grade. You know too much about me."

"Funny I don't think I know enough," he said. "You haven't told me what happened in seventh grade. But am I the only one besides him that knows that you aren't an iron clad snow bitch?"

"Mark knows I am."

"That's why you want me gone. I've seen parts of you others haven't."

"I have no idea what you're talking about," I replied smugly piling my unfolded clothes in my basket. Tuck pushed me to the wall against the dryers trapping me again.

"You're human."

"That's never been proven."

"Let me come upstairs and I'll prove it to you."

I scoffed at his insane ramblings.

"There are worse things in the world than letting yourself become vulnerable to another person. How about I make a deal with you?"

"What's that?"

"I'll let you tie me up—"

"I'm not here for your sick fantasies."

"I'll be completely at your will." His finger traced along my neck.

"I can do whatever I want to you?"

"Within reason."

"No dildos up the ass?" I joked.

"I'd appreciate if that rule stayed in place."

"Did we have our first fight?"

"If it makes you happy. Katie, why didn't you just tell me?" he asked walking me upstairs holding my hand and carrying my basket on his hip. "It makes sense because what that guy did to you was wrong. Way wrong."

We sat down on my futon.

"That's why you put the rules in place. Because you weren't going to let yourself fall prey to someone like him again."

I kept my face firm more to hold in tears than possibly show emotion.

"You know you've probably missed out on some great guys. And that's why you don't have any girlfriends."

Tuck was great at reading my mind but got annoyed when I didn't confirm his theories.

"You're not friends with girls because they wouldn't understand your rules."

The lump had reemerged in my throat.

"You don't like Mark's girl because you're afraid when he's in a relationship, things get shared. Although you trust him, there's a part of you afraid Carrie might find out about you."

"He proved tonight he can't be trusted."

"Why? Because he knows I love and care for you? That he didn't want you to throw this away with your stupid behavior." Tuck's hand swung between the two of us to indicate what I almost lost.

"It wasn't just that. Remember when you said it didn't make sense I wasn't scared getting lost with you."

"Um, yes, you said you trusted me."

"How many guys have told you they've been with me?"

"A few, but they aren't ones you've been with."

"You sure?"

"Yes. I think I know who on campus you've been with."

"Okay," I replied, knowing at least one he'll never know about. "My gut's pretty good. With you I instantly felt safe. There is something about Carrie that makes my stomach turn. I've liked a few of Mark's girlfriends, but she's not right."

"You got issues. Everyone has issues. Yours are compounded by a father who won't let you make a mistake. Does your father carry malpractice insurance?"

"Yes."

"Why?"

I shook my head not wanting to have this conversation.

"He's. Not. Perfect."

"Insurance is a safety net. It doesn't indicate flaws."

"Shit happens. What happened to you was bad. I don't want you to think I don't think it wasn't, but worse things have happened to people and they didn't just shut down."

"How did I shut down? My grades didn't drop, I was still in all my activities—"

"Just because you were present in your life doesn't mean you were there. Katie, you kept yourself from enjoying everything. Did you even like sex or were you trying to distance yourself from Clark."

Crossing my arms I closed my eyes and held tight hoping he'd drop it.

"Do you? Answer me." He pushed and pushed, and I could feel the pressure building in my head and gut. "Because if you don't like it, we won't do it anymore. I like you, Katie. Your body's a bonus."

"I liked it. It didn't hurt like I thought it would at first. I like it."

"But you don't want to, because how sick of a person are you to not be completely crushed and turned off after what he did to you."

"I didn't know at the time."

"And that's why you liked it."

"I suppose. Can we stop talking now?"

"Why? This is the first time we talked and it's just me putting words in your mouth because you don't want to talk."

"Then let's stop, okay." I leaned back.

"You got a little freak in you, but you're ashamed. Does your daddy know what you do?"

"Why would he?" I questioned.

"You live in a world where you live and die by your father's approval and you find pleasure in something he doesn't approve of. What does Kyle do?"

"Men and small farm animals."

"Cut the sarcasm. What does he do for a living?"

"Writes, well he's a waiter because he hasn't gotten picked up yet."

"And your other siblings?"

"Kimberly is a pediatric orthopedist, Kenneth is a cardiothorasic surgeon and Kevin is finishing up a stint with Doctors Without Borders."

"Kevin's your dad's second least favorite, isn't he?"

I turned to him and wished he wasn't so good at reading people.

"How did you know?"

"Kyle went against his wishes completely, Kevin followed suit, but took it in a direction your father doesn't respect. The hippie route."

"Not necessarily." Here I was about to stick up for my father's pecking order knowing full well I'd been afraid my whole life of being on the wrong end of the rankings.

"The jury's still out on you because you are following the right path, but until you complete your residency and start your own practice or join his you're a flight risk. Kyle's your favorite because he openly rebelled on everything."

"Maybe."

"Do the rest of the KKK do that?"

"Not funny. My dad's name is Kenneth and so he just wanted all K names after Ken Jr. was born."

"Yeah, that's why you're bringing me home for the holidays." His eyebrow rose in challenge.

"Who said I was going home?"

"You're staying here?"

"I haven't decided. I wasn't invited."

"Home? You need to be invited home? For the holidays?"

"Yes. You don't just show up in my family."

His mouth dropped, aghast by family protocol. It's just the way it is. They don't surprise me, and I don't surprise them.

"We could leave right now and be at my parents' house in like four hours and we'd be welcomed in and fed supper."

"Without calling ahead?"

"Crazy, isn't it. My mom would be happy to see me."

"We schedule everything. Any adjustments need to be approved."

"What if you need a weekend away from college?"

"I'd probably crash at Mark's."

"At his dorm room. That's not an escape."

"His penthouse overlooking Lake Michigan. It's an escape. Sixty stories up in the Hancock Building. He's got two levels."

"Wow. I feel you're not the only one with secrets."

"Every family hides details."

"What's the family gossip? I have a feeling Kyle gave you an earful the other night."

I leaned forward and thought about all of the juicy tidbits Kyle filled me in on. He was everyone's favorite because he didn't judge us. Loving us and taking us for what we are.

"Kimberly smokes pot. Ken Jr's on his fourth mistress. And Katherine the daughter whose name comes from the Greek meaning pure is a slut."

"No, you're not. A slut doesn't have rules."

"Funny."

"And if you would have talked about your past, this situation tonight could have been avoided."

"Talking to anyone but Mark is hard for me."

"I want to know about you and Mark."

"Are you jealous?"

"No. But there has to be more to the two of you than a seventh grade romance. You all are tight as dick's hatbands."

"That's a disgusting allegory," I said shaking my head. "How can I word this? Um… He's a trust fund baby. In the traditional sense."

"Aren't you a trust fund baby?"

"My dad's a surgeon with five kids. Three he put through medical school and one he will be putting through medical school. He has three ex-wives and although he's set up minor trust funds for all of us, I am on skid row compared to Mark."

"Mark doesn't sound like a trust fund name."

"His real name is Clifton Marcus Lystrom the IV." I drug out his moniker stressing each name.

"He's a Lystrom?" Tuck asked amazed. "As in the Lystrom Group? Lystrom Hall? The art department?"

"That's him. Only admin knows his name. He's going by his mother's maiden name, Kloski. When he graduates and has his real name read, people are going to shit their pants."

"What does that have to do with why you are friends? And why would Richie Rich be going to college for nursing?"

"He wanted to keep hanging out with me and he's got this pure heart. That's why I hate Carrie. He made the mistake of flying her to New York on his private plane on their second date. She sees him, she sees dollars. Look, he was raised by the nanny…true trust funder. His parents died when he was seven, but even before that they were only in town a few times a year.

"We joke about seventh grade, but we became friends years before that. My mother was all about appearances. My father looks for perfection in all he deems family. Mark and I had mommy and me classes together."

"I thought his parents weren't around."

"They weren't. He was more nanny and me. But then his parents got me into the Carmichael Academy for grade school and we stayed friends because he's always been scrawny and tenderhearted. In elementary he was picked on a lot."

"And you protected him."

"Until around fifth grade when material possessions and parents let the kids know Mark was the kid to be friends with. In Junior High he threw a party and learned I was the only one that liked him, the person."

"Like when I was sick." Tuck rubbed between my shoulder blades. "He's not the only tenderhearted one."

"Anyway. That's when we got serious for about two weeks. It was the physical part of our relationship that let us know we were best friends. After we broke up, we made a pact that we'd always look out for each other. Not that we listen every time. Like right now with Carrie."

"The physical part of your relationship is the only reason why you're not together?"

"Attraction is a big part of a relationship. You're the first person I've trusted besides him."

"So I'm him with the physical."

I crawled over to him and straddled his hips. "For now."

"What does that mean?"

"That means that hopefully someday you'll be more."

"Is someone getting romantic on me?"

"And now I'm leaving." Crawling away he caught me and held me close.

"Kiss me."

"No."

"Are you saying someday you want me to be your—"

I kissed him long and hard. Not letting him up for air. He knew I hated the N-word and anytime he really wanted a kiss he'd learned in just a few weeks he could get me to latch on like I was nearing death without his touch.

"I love you, Katie. Mark will always be in your life, wont he?"

"We're a package deal."

"Good. You're both good people. Now that I know more about him, I understand why he's your friend. Most guys in his position would be getting high and partying in Hollywood or New York. Instead he's finding his own way."

"It's easy to do with a safety net."

"That does help."

"You can't tell anyone. He doesn't want anyone to know. I'm afraid Carrie will spill soon because I've heard the girls around her asking why she's with him. At least he hasn't told her his name, I think. It's annoying people acting like she some hot thing and he's the creature from the black lagoon. He's cute in his own way and she'd be pretty if she got rid of that thing on her face."

"What thing?"

"Her personality."

He burst out in laughter.

"It keeps her face in a constant sneer. You ever noticed that?"

"I love when you're petty, but tell me this, why is it okay for people to know you're a trust fund baby, but not him?"

"They don't know, they assume. Plus there are less male gold-diggers than female."

"I'm only with you because of your money, you know that right?"

"Of course. That's why I pussy whipped you before I let you know about the cash."

"Oh, I knew."

"Did you?"

"No."

CHAPTER SEVENTEEN

Mondays sucked. Okay, Mondays and Wednesdays sucked because all of the football players had study hall. Tuck would be stuck in the basement of the library for two hours after dinner.

I decided I'd walk with him to the library under the illusion I would spend a few hours studying.

"You really have two hours of homework?"

"Maybe. Maybe I'll walk by the study rooms and flash you."

"That wouldn't be advisable. We study in groups of ten."

We sat on the couches by the entrance his hand holding mine stroking his thumb on the back of my hand. Cuddled up next to him I didn't feel uncomfortable instead it was the way I liked it to be. Next to him, having the warmth of his body against mine.

"Fine. You're coming over to my room after?" I asked.

"For a little bit. You've been exhausting me. It's easy for you. You just have to roll over and go to sleep." He placed a soft kiss on the crown of my head. "I have to go back to my dorm."

"But then I toss and turn because you're not there."

He kissed me again, this time on my lips, but we were interrupted by a thunderous roar. Leaving his forehead leaning against mine he smiled at me. "I think they're here."

"Bastards. I guess I'll study history, but you have to help me with anatomy later tonight."

"You suck at being coy and seductive."

"I know. But Mark's still with his grandmother in Chicago so someone has to be there for me." He gave me one quick peck then got up and followed the crowd downstairs, the guys ribbing him all the way. He took it in stride then looked over his shoulder and winked at me making my body warm.

Getting up I went to a computer and entered a few key words. Suggestions came up and I wrote down their codes so I could find the books I needed. Then I decided I needed something without academic purposes. My dirty little secret. Vampire sex novels. I went upstairs and perused the section hoping to find anything to could get me through these stupid study halls.

Then I went downstairs into the stacks. Single study rooms were against the eastern wall while the group rooms were on the western. Down the center were periodicals. Thumbing along the way I was searching for the *New England Journal of Medicine*.

An annoying laugh made me come to the end of the row. I peered over the edge to see a flash of curly blond standing at the door of a single study room. Around her waist a hand pulled her back into the room.

Looking at who could only be Carrie I tried to come to a reason for her to be studying, she was stupid as hell so that is a possibility. The hand was my issue. She fell out of the room again and her disheveled shirt was only half tucked. I watched her hand softly stroke the face of a guy. Her lips locking on his making my blood pressure rise.

"I knew it," I snapped as I crossed to her. "You cheating whore."

"Back off, Katie. This has nothing to do with you."

"No, it has to do with Mark who's nursing his damn grandmother while you're here giving lessons in anatomy to—to—" I stared at him but couldn't place the face. "Who are you?"

"Tyrone."

"Right, Tyrone. You won't even let Mark slip his hand under your shirt you born again hypocrite."

She pushed me back into a row then glanced at Tyrone.

"Black guys don't count."

"What?" Rage stepped up to a level I couldn't comprehend. My adrenaline raced and my hand shook. Breathing in deep I stilled my hand. You cannot cut a person open with hands that shake. Unfortunately, my head had not calmed down. It kept running over what she had said.

"Black guys don't settle down and start families, so they don't count."

"So because you're a racist it's okay to have sex with black guys, but not white because you'd hate to have them think you're easy. I knew you were stupid, but I didn't know you were delusional."

"Lower your voice. You're going to cause a scene."

"You'll be lucky if a scene is the only thing I do. I knew you were a piece of shit since the first day."

"Please, we both know that you'd never marry Tuck. Why you're dating him in public I'll never know."

"I don't know what I'm going to do with Tuck in the future, but I haven't ruled out any possibility with him. That's why I'm dating him. Exclusively. You do know what exclusively means, right. It's what Mark thinks he has with you."

"Right that's why he went back to Chicago, I know what he's really doing."

"What? Working off the blue balls you gave him? I don't think so. He really has a grandmother and she's really in the hospital."

"Whatever. Just because you want to live in a world of make believe doesn't mean I have to. When are you taking Tuck to meet your family?"

"When I have family worthy enough of him! You're breaking up with Mark when he gets back to town."

"Then hell I am."

"Fine I'll just tell him what I saw."

"He wouldn't believe you. Do I look like a girl who would stoop so low to date a black guy?"

At this point I believe I blacked out. Maybe my blood sugar dropped or spiked. Or I had some out of body experience. I don't know if it was her blatant racism or the fact she had been fucking over my friend for months now, but something built up in me so great not even the sound created from the crack of her left orbital bone woke me. It wasn't until sometime later when I finally saw Tuck's eyes and felt his hand stroking back my hair I truly woke up.

"What happened?" I asked through the cotton mouth, yeah, I needed to check my glucose level.

"Stick with that baby girl, you may actually get the insanity defense."

"No, really, I don't know what happened after the nasally whore said something about stooping down low to date a black guy." Glancing at my hand I visualized light bruising and scrapes. Looking up into Tuck's sweet brown eyes I could see worry behind them.

"You really blacked out?"

"It might be my sugars."

"Sugars? More secrets."

Shit, I'd hid my diabetes from him.

"Later, but yes, I blacked out. Are you done with study hall already?" Tuck peered behind me then to the side that's when I saw a crowd and, in the middle of it, were two campus security officers and Carrie with an ice pack on her cheek. "What happened?"

"That's what we'd like to know," one of the overweight, balding officers asked.

"I don't remember. I caught her having sex in a study room—and then it all's like a blur."

"You attacked me you maniac," Carrie cried.

"So she was having sex in a study room. With who?" the officer asked.

"Tyrone," I replied.

"Are you dating Tyrone?" he questioned.

"No, I've never seen him before."

"Then why did you attack her?"

"She's dating my best friend and she kept saying things that pissed me off."

"Like what?" The genius security guard's face scrunched in confusion.

"That sleeping with black men doesn't count because they never settle down and start families."

"And this upset you why?"

"Because I'm human." Tuck squeezed my hand and I could see him out of the corner of my eye smiling. "Look, press charges or let me go. It was an adrenaline rush, mixed with my diabetes and now I have a headache."

"It's up to her to press charges."

"Hell, yeah, I'm pressing charges," Carrie howled. "You're a vicious animal."

"And you're a whoring slut."

"Hey." Tuck placed his hand on my chest. "I'm not breaking you two apart again."

"Again?"

"Yes, we heard the fight, I saw you so I yanked you off her."

I leaned against his shoulder so I could whisper. "Why didn't you get me out of here?"

"Someone already called security," he replied. "They caught me."

"Bastards."

"Hey," the guard interjected.

"Not you the tattle tale."

"You can't just go around beating everyone." Rent-a-cop Randy gave me a hard scowl as if it would shame me.

"I don't want to beat everyone. I just want to beat her. And press

147

charges. It'll make it easier for Mark to dump you with the evidence you were getting banged in a study room."

"It was a blow job." She sneered as if the act made it better.

"I heard white girls give the best ones," Tuck whispered, and I backhanded his chest. "What? You said it."

CHAPTER EIGHTEEN

Tuck walked me back to the dorm. Kissing my right fist that apparently had been used in the attack on Carrie. It was still a blur, but who knows if that's the way it will stay in court a month from now.

"She's not answering," the girl at the desk said as Mark leaned against it.

"I suppose I should tell him now." My head hurt and the thought of talking to Mark was overwhelming me. It was like I had run a marathon my muscles were so weak. The adrenaline had really done a number on me.

"Hey, you need to rest and check your sugar," Tuck said.

"I'm not infirmed, it's just diabetes. I can wait until I'm done with Mark."

"Do you have the stuff to make cookies?" he asked. Tuck had discovered baking was my calming technique.

"Yes. I don't think…"

"This is a man to man conversation. Anything you say will be taken wrong." For the first time I was really glad to have Tuck around to handle the hard stuff. I always had to handle that myself.

"Hey, guys, what's up?" Mark asked as he turned around.

"Why don't you come on up to Katie's room?" Tuck offered.

"Sure. Carrie must still be studying."

"Grandma's better?" I asked.

"Yes, your dad moved her to a floor bed this morning. She's trying to decide where in the Mediterranean to recuperate," he joked.

"Sounds like her."

"Yeah. Seconds from death and now back to bossing us around. Even your dad she treats like a five-year-old."

"It's character building," I said as I grabbed my baking supplies, blood tester and headed to the kitchen.

"What's going on?'

"Making cookies."

"The two of you look like you were hit by a bus." Mark's head bounced between Tuck and me. Only made worse because I couldn't look him in the eye. I hated being this right.

Heading down to the dorm kitchen I dug for the mixer and cookie sheets. My eyes started to get wet with tears while my body shook. How I could be depressed with chocolate chip cookies baking I'll never know.

It took three sticks to get my blood onto the testing strip and low and behold I was at fifty. Syringes had been part of my life since grade school. Still my level was bordering on dangerous as I drew out my insulin and gave myself a dose. Sitting in the nineteen seventies reject chairs around the table I popped a few chocolate chips in my mouth.

A few warm cookies later my sugar had rebounded, but I was still drained emotionally.

Washing the bowl while the last batch cooked, I decided I wanted cinnamon cookies too. Really, I didn't want to go back to my room. I'm not sure Mark had left by now.

"I knew I smelled something good." It was Keyondra and Trinity. "Hey, Katie."

"You want a cookie?" I asked while measuring the last of my flour.

"Yes, please." Trinity grabbed three and sat on the counter. "Tell me truthfully, how long have you and Tuck been together?"

I sighed and finished mixing the dough. My face flushed and a knot began to form in my gut. My body couldn't handle the drama today.

"Officially. The Sunday after you asked me to talk to him. Unofficially a few weeks before that."

"Why didn't you just tell me that?" Keyondra asked.

"Tell you what?"

"That you liked him."

"We weren't like that." I dropped my head and laughed. "He was in my room with the flu that night."

"He spend the night a lot," Trinity sneered. "Or just when he's sick."

"I plead the fifth."

"You're cute together. The two of you," Keyondra said.

"I don't like it. It makes my stomach turn," Trinity added.

"It didn't stop you from eating a half dozen cookies," I said under my breath.

I dropped the last spoonfuls of cinnamon cookie batter on a cookie sheet. Then pulled out the last batch of chocolate chip swapping my fresh sheet into the oven. I was trying to avoid the acid building in my throat from her statement.

"Did you hear me?"

"How do you want me to respond?" I asked glaring at her before checking my watch. "Thanks. I'm sure our children will be beautiful as long as God doesn't strike us down for comingling."

"I didn't mean to—"

"What are we doing wrong? Is it because you liked him or because I'm white? Would you be just as upset if he was dating Keyondra?"

"Who said I'm upset?" Trinity growled.

"Why don't you approve of us?"

"There aren't many good black men out there."

"There are more than you give credit to."

"What's that supposed to mean?"

"Hey, baby." Tuck came in cutting off the discussion. "Got those cookies done yet?"

"I started a second batch of cinnamon cookies."

"Cinnamon?"

"You'll like them," I said using the spatula to slide the last of the chocolate chip cookies off on to the parchment paper.

"I'm sure I will," he said, snagged a warm cookie popping it in his mouth. With a full mouth he turned toward Trinity. "You're in my Abnormal Psych class, right?" At least that's what I think he said through the cookie.

"Yes."

"You friends?" he asked pointing between the two of us.

I looked at Trinity, while balancing on the side of my feet then turned around and started to wash dishes.

"Of course," Trinity said, I could hear the smile on her face and the fake sweet tone she was using.

"That's why she's always popping up when you're around. Because we're friends." I grumbled and kept my back turned to all of them.

"Should we stay in your room from now on?"

"Yes."

"Did I interrupt something?" Tuck finally asked.

"We make Trinity want to vomit." I held back my tears. Something I didn't expect to have formed. Damn hormone spikes.

"Is she the one eating all the cookies?" Tuck pointed out.

He knew full well who she was. That was a double dig for me. I'm really liking being part of a couple. It's nice to have someone who has your back. He grabbed a towel and started to dry the dishes I had washed.

"We need to get these up to Mark."

"How is he?"

"Not good." We had officially started our own conversation excluding the girls that don't approve of us. "He may still be curled in the fetal position."

"That's why I made the cinnamon cookies." I turned around to see almost all of my chocolate chip cookies were gone. Putting the cooled cookies in my *Tupperware* I shook my head. "I asked if you wanted one not one dozen. Why would you want my cookies anyway? Is there a female on this campus that isn't a hypocrite?"

"One," Tuck replied wrapping his arms around my waist snagging a cinnamon cookie before I put the lid on my *Tupperware*. "Keep your damn opinions to yourself next time," Tuck warned the girls. "She's not the reason I'm not with you. I'll enlighten you sometime if you'd like to know why."

"Who said I wanted you?" Trinity snapped. "You worthless—"

I glared at her, literally biting my tongue with my K-9 tooth to control myself.

"Augh." She huffed out of the room.

"Bye Tuck. Thanks, Katie, for the cookies," Keyondra said as she ran behind her.

"You're pretty awesome you know that?"

"I've heard," he replied giving me a light peck on my forehead.

CHAPTER NINETEEN

The shine on the red Christmas wrapping paper flashed as I rounded the corner to the lobby of my dorm. I'd say a good four inches around the cube tied with a shimmering golden bow.

"Did you go to the mall and have them wrap this for you?" I questioned Tuck feeling the deceptively light gift and giving it a little shake.

"Why would you think that?"

"Because I'm used to Mark's gifts that are wrapped in the same slap happy style he used in second grade."

"Well, my mother happens to be a step removed from Martha Stewart," he said. "Now open it."

Popping the side tape I wasn't about to tear the beautiful paper. Tuck crossed his arms and rolled his eyes at my delicate technique.

"It's not Mittens."

"My cat?" I questioned.

"Yes, tear it open like a warm loaf of bread."

I stopped and turned my eyes to him. "One time, my sugar was low."

"A ravaging beast would have left the loaf in better condition."

"They're carnivores."

"Find a rabid raccoon then."

I slowed my opening of the gift. Drawing out the tape removal to a painfully tedious task until even I couldn't take the pace. Finally cleared of paper I saw a brown box labeled with stir sticks. It was a full box of swizzle sticks for me.

"I thought you'd need them."

"Because of finals?" I questioned.

"Because I want to take you home with me over break."

"Oh." I crossed to a couch in the lobby and sat. "The whole two weeks?"

"Ideally." He intertwined his fingers with mine. "You were pretty frustrated when you went home for Thanksgiving."

"My dad took call at the hospital. He'll spend most of it answering the ER's pages. Didn't make since."

"Well then why not come home with me?"

"Meeting the parents."

"Among others."

"Others?" I questioned. "Your brothers will be home."

"Yep. Titus and Magnus."

"Couldn't your mother have stopped your father in his sick and twisted Roman naming rituals?"

"Your father got past three women with the K-Krew."

"Good point." I slipped a straw from my gift and absently began knotting it for the legs. "Guess a history professor isn't going to have a reason to not be there for the holiday."

"Nope." His finger plucked my would be stick figure from my hands. "And my mom loves holidays."

"By loves…" my voice trailed off wondering if it meant more than a haphazard tree tossed up sometime the week of Christmas. That had been my holiday for the past handful or so years.

"There will be homemade eggnog, a retelling of A Christmas Carol and—"

"Don't say it," I warned.

"We will not be caroling outside the house, but inside there might be a few rounds of *Jingle Bells* and *This Christmas*."

"*This Christmas*?"

His eyes widened in surprise at my lack of Christmas carol knowledge. "Okay baby girl, this season you will OD on the Christmas spirit."

"Bah—" His lips found mine silencing my fear and doubt, thus ending any discussion. This year my break would be spent in Kentucky.

A week later Tuck had my keys spinning on his index finger waiting for me to finish loading my suitcases. "Are you sure they want me for a full two weeks? My father doesn't even want me for a full two weeks."

"Actually they just didn't want to pay for the train ticket home so once you drop me off you can leave."

"See that makes sense to me."

"You are a twisted, messed up woman."

"True, but I am yours which means you picked me. What does that make you?"

"I doubt the DSM-5 has addressed my issues yet."

"True." Buckled in I turned to him. "East, right? You know where you're going, right?"

"Do you trust me?"

The loaded question crashed against my already stressed nerves. I'd met parents in my lifetime. Random ones, with little need for them to like me after a play date. If they did, bonus, but I wasn't one to put on the love me vibe. Did I own that vibe?

"What a girl won't do—"

"Yes, sorry," I said cutting him off when I realized I'd been lost in my own thoughts for far too long. Trust came with being part of a whole and like it or not when I was with Tuck, I was whole. The feeling was foreign, scary and made me wonder why on most nights I could sleep more than four-hours.

"Left out of the parking lot," he prodded.

"That's east?"

"It's a one-way street."

"I know that," I practically spat at him. "I was testing you."

"Uh-huh." He smirked.

Three hours later, I wound my way through a neighborhood of homes. Manicured lawns sported plastic reindeer and snowmen. Nativity crèches had spotlights shining in the manger. One home was lit, slightly under *National Lampoon* levels. Tuck was right, his mother was a Martha Stewart. The lighting was tastefully done. Bows of holly and wreaths festooned the home. White lights twinkled around the windows frosted over with fake snow.

"Do I need to guess?" I asked slowing by the Christmas lighthouse of a home.

"Wait until we get inside," he said as I pulled up along the curb.

While we were unloading our suitcases his parents came to the door. His father fit the mold of a history professor. Light gray beard, slightly balding wearing a button-down shirt with a sweater over the top. Taller like Tuck he had broad shoulders and a slight pot belly. His mother in contrast was trim in a sweater set and mom jeans.

"Augustus Tuckman, you little sneak," she cried right as two large men barreled out of the house and tackled Tuck on the front lawn. "You didn't say you were coming home for Christmas."

"Did I need to?" he questioned from a headlock.

"No, but I would have made up the spare bedroom for your friend."

"Like—" Tuck tapped his brother's arm demanding release. "It's not always ready, besides I was hoping my room was still available."

"For you," she scolded as she crossed the lawn to me. "Not for your friend. Should I assume you are Katie?"

"Yes." I swallowed and extended my hand only to be pulled into a hug.

"Gus talks about you all the time when he calls home."

"Does he now."

"Of course." She released me from the hug, then wrapped her arm around my shoulder. "Now, he said you love Shirley Temple. Is he trying to make you out to be a sweet angel and lyin' to me?"

The slight Southern twang of her voice caught me off guard since Tuck didn't have a trace of an accent.

"Boring dinners growing up listening to speakers."

"No babysitters for you."

"Few and far between."

Tuck's brothers were the next to overwhelm me and by the time I was placing my bag in the spare room I collapsed on the bed from the social overload. My eyes drooped and the world floated away.

"What you won't do to get out of a cutthroat game of Spades."

The bed dipped and I struggled to open my eyes. "Huh?"

"Was the ride too much?" he asked, brushing my hair back from my cheek and tugging me next to him. The natural reaction to curl against his body and nuzzle into the crook of his shoulder was involuntary

"I'm sorry." I yawned trying to remember where I was. "What time is it?"

"After midnight. I needed to wait until my parents went to sleep."

"Didn't your mom say we couldn't sleep together?"

"My mom also wanted me to wait until I got married to have sex. I'm nothing if not a bastion of disappointment."

"I doubt that."

"You think they wanted me to be a football player?"

"Looking at the size of your brothers I think you all were grown in a lab."

"Magnus—"

"The oldest, right?" I questioned.

"Yes. Magnus is on track to finish his PhD in the Classics."

"What is that?"

"A combo of Latin, Hebrew and Greek. All studied free, for us, at my dad's school."

"But you don't pay for college, do you?"

"A little, there are no free rides at a school our size." His hand slid under my shirt and brushed along my belly. "Aren't you over dressed for bed?"

"Seriously? Your mom—"

"Raised three boys and is under no delusion about who we are." Tuck rolled on top of me.

A soft brush of his lips along the column of my neck had me biting mine. Did he actually think I'd have sex with him?

"Shhhh," he whispered in my ear. "Don't make a sound."

"Oh, no, you—"

He found my lips silencing me. The silent love making was the most erotic in my life. Holding in my screams. The slow, dragging pace of his entry and retreat. Biting his shoulder each time I climaxed. Clawing his back and having him hiss in satisfaction before burying himself deep inside me.

When I woke in the morning my bed was empty and my body sore. Just like the dorms we were sneaking around making sure not to get caught. Only this time the naughtiness had a sexy edge that had me crawling out of bed in search of Tuck.

Properly primped I made my way to the kitchen. A mix of morning smells hit me when I reached the doorway. My stomach grumbled loud enough to have the whole Tuckman family turn.

"Bacon gets me every time," I said twisting my fingers together.

"Morning. Are you a coffee drinker?" his mother asked with a tone in her voice that made me wonder if she knew everything about last night.

For the next few days I was inundated with cookies, caroling and vicious board games. Even though Tuck and his brother Titus were the athletes in the home, the competitive gene had to be in the blood. Each night, but Christmas Eve, Tuck slipped into my room and in the morning I was alone.

Christmas morning was magical though. Woken with a cup of cocoa and a kiss, Tuck sat on the side of my bed in pajamas with a backdoor and slippers.

"Where are the bunny ears?" I giggled then blew on my drink. "Can't believe they make those in your size. Or for men."

"Oh, they make them in all sorts of sizes."

My eyes widened as a matching flannel one was placed on my pillow.

"Very funny," I rebuked the horrifying image.

"Nope, you'd look weird if you weren't wearing them and I know how you hate to stand out."

"I'm white, I already stand out."

"Not really. Hate to break it to you, Katie Gills, you're black by injection."

"I didn't get mine last night." I bumped his shoulder with mine. "Wait, what time is it?"

"O' Dark Thirty my love. Christmas does not wait for the sun to rise in this home."

"I'm going back to sleep. Wake me when it's time for presents."

"I am."

"Dear lord," I balked turning to see a clock reading way too damn early in the morning.

"Put on those pajamas or I'll be hard pressed to not give you a good start to your day." He stood. "See you downstairs."

"Tease," I called as he unbuttoned one of the barn door buttons and flashed me as he walked out.

True to his word every member of the Tuckman family was adorned in flannel, footie pajamas and Titus the youngest wore a Santa hat. Personally, I was very impressive to get a junior in high school to play along.

"'Bout time sleepy head," Titus said. "You don't have siblings, do you?"

"Actually I have four."

"Do you not know the time honored tradition of rushing down the stairs for your presents?" he questioned. "Knocking over the bigger ones by undercutting them and tapping their knees."

"I'm sorry I missed that." Snuggling next to Tuck he slid his arm around my hip.

"Yeah, I regret teaching him that trick," Tuck admitted. "Now, presents."

"The last thing our guest needs to think is I've raised a bunch of heathens."

"It's been wonderful here this year. Right now I'd be—well sleeping, but when I woke up, I'd be reheating pizza."

"You said you have siblings," his mother responded, probably happy I'd finally divulged a little morsel about myself.

"Yeah, but outside of my brother Kyle no one consistently lived with me and, well my other siblings celebrated with their mothers."

"What about your mother?"

"She passed when I was young. Either way it's hard to celebrate with half a family around."

"Well, you're our guest so you get your stocking and a present to open first."

"Seriously." Titus' face dropped and his eyes cut to a green and silver package by his thigh. "This job sucks."

A generic stocking had been hung for me and was now filled with candy, an orange and a copy of *The Addams Family*. Although I received the first gift everyone had one before we all opened ours together. Mine of course was from Tuck.

Removing the GPS he got me from the box I began fiddling with it. Two addresses were saved. The college and his parents' home.

"No matter what you'll be able to find your way home and to me," he said brushing his lips along the back of my neck. "Never again will you be lost."

CHAPTER TWENTY

"Katie Gills." The drone over the intercom sounded bored with the world in general today.

"Yes."

"You have an escort. He's requesting you lock up your room when you come down."

"Okay." Snatching my keys, I walked down the stairs to see Tuck smiling. "What's going on?"

"Can I see your keys?"

"Sure." I tossed them to him and followed their path to his other hand. "Where we goin'?"

Being part of a couple I'd loosened up when it came to unplanned outings. Last spring I learned what fun can come from unexpected adventures.

"Do you trust me?"

"That's a loaded question," I warned, and he pulled out a necktie. Glancing down at my pajama pants and his old football jersey, I sighed. "Am I dressed appropriately?"

"I've got clothes for you," he said wrapping the tie around my eyes blinding me.

"Tuck," I warned as nerves made my stomach tumble. "I can't do—"

"I know it's Tuesday, but I thought we got away from the rules last fall."

"It's not that." His hand slid into mine.

"Would I hurt you?" He stroked my hand that was currently at the epicenter of my full body quake. "Katie Gills, if I've shown you nothing since we met it's that I won't hurt you."

"I don't like surprises."

"You haven't liked a lot of things until I've shown you." He had a point. "Walk slowly I'll tell you when there's a step."

We walked to the car and by the time we reached it I had actually moved to a normal pace having become comfortable with his directions. Reaching up to take off the blindfold resulted in a stern warning and my hands being placed on my lap.

"Why would bringing you to your car be the surprise?"

"You could have it filled with something tasty or balloons or is there a puppy in here?"

"No. Now behave and don't mess with that again."

I have no idea how long the ride took, in reality for me it had been twelve days, sixteen hours, forty-three minutes and seven seconds. Tuck said it was about twenty-five minutes. In my head I tried to calculate what cities were twenty-five minutes away, but the pounding headache I had from my frustration got in the way.

"You want something for your headache?" Tuck asked shaking a pill bottle in front of me.

"How did you—"

"I know you, Katie, whether you want to admit it or not."

"Then you should know I'm not taking any pill without first looking at it."

"Because I'm likely to slip you a mickie?"

I sat silently on my hands trying to make my fear go away.

"I'm getting out."

"Don't leave me," I yelped.

"May I start again? I'm getting out so I can help you walk to where we're going. Can you please not mess with the blindfold?"

"You've got thirty seconds."

"Is that a real thirty seconds or Katie super fast counting seconds?"

"The latter."

"When my door closes you can start."

The door creaked slightly, and a soft breeze wafted across my cheek. I waited, a pit forming in my stomach, for the door to close. What is he doing? Tying his shoe? Admiring the view?

"Are you going—" It was at that moment my door opened and I screamed. "Don't do that!" I yelled. "You scared the crap out of me." My hands reached for him. "Where are you so I can hit you?"

"Right here," he whispered in my ear.

"That wasn't funny," I pouted.

His lips brushed along the column of my neck. "Forgive me?"

"Never."

"Forgive me or this will have all been for nothing. I'll take you back right now."

"I hate you."

"I know. I didn't ask you to like me, just forgive me."

"Fine."

"I'll take that."

"That's all you're getting."

"We'll see."

Walking me into a building I could hear light murmuring, but nothing more. His hand was secure to my waist and I leaned into his body. He was practically carrying me. I heard a bell and we stepped on what I soon determined was an elevator.

Then down a hall I assume. It was stuffy and felt more confined, but that could be the blindfold. Another softer beep and I heard a door open. A few more steps and Tuck stepped back making me reach for him again.

"You want the blindfold off?"

"Yes!" He removed it and we were in a hotel room. There was a king size bed and an in room whirlpool. On the table was a vase full of red and white roses with a pint of strawberries and a container of whip cream.

"I'm having dinner brought up later."

"You think that I'm going to…" His lips were on mine as his hands went to my hips to lift me off the ground and carry me to the bed. "Why are we here?"

"I'm hurt. You don't remember."

"Remember what?" I scanned my mind thinking we weren't together until after Homecoming so it's not our anniversary.

Getting up he crossed the room and pulled out a small bag. "One year ago today you said if I was still in your rotation, I could buy you something." The handles of the bag rested nicely on his finger as he swung it back and forth. "Now I know technically your rotation has ceased to exist. It has, right?" I grabbed a pillow and threw it at his head. "I'll take that as a yes. But I'm still here and it's been a year. I know I marked in my calendar as the best day ever."

"Has it really been a year?"

"Yes. Now pay up."

I pulled out the thong and teddy. "Why do want me in this?"

"I was going to get you some high heels with feathers on them, but that was two days ago not today. I still want to see that pillow fight."

"Nobody wants to see me in this."

"Katie, I need to tell you something," Tuck's face became serious. "My real name is Nobody and if I don't see you in that in the next five minutes—"

"I have a headache."

He tossed me the ibuprofen bottle. "Have a strawberry so you don't upset your stomach."

"Are we getting into the whirlpool? If so then—"

"Thong! Now!" he ordered pointing to the bathroom.

In a huff I went to the bathroom and put the stupid thing on. Nervously I walked out of the room poking my head out first.

"Are you sure?" I asked as he sat in the chair next to the table.

His finger extended then reached behind him and Barry White started to sing *Can't Get Enough of Your Love.*

His deep voice flowed out of the stereo *"I've heard people say that too much of anything is not good for you."*

"Are you serious?"

"Come on." He leaned over, resting his elbows on his knees and slapping his hands together rubbing them like it would warm me up. "You're smiling," he teased, and I was. Biting my bottom lip and smiling so hard it hurt.

Grasping the doorjamb with all my might I extended my right leg and heard an ooohhh yeah. Then I let myself fall back a little and curved my body out still holding on to the doorjamb like it was a stripper pole. My hair fell down almost touching the floor until I whipped myself back up.

"That's what I'm talkin' about. Get over here, girl," Tuck growled. I released my death grip and strode over to him trying my best cat like skills. Tuck leaned back in his chair and I straddled his hips. His hands went to my ass squeezing hard as his head whipped around to get a better view.

With my knees firmly planted on either side of him on the chair I extended my body up so my stomach was right on his lips. He took one hand and pulled up the smooth nylon of the teddy over his head with a light kiss, followed by a lick my body melted into his arms.

His other hand went to the middle of my back as a brace and I fell back into his arm. This caused his lips to travel south from my belly button to the top of my thong. He lifted us up and my legs wrapped around his waist. Carried to the bed he laid me out.

"You're right," he purred in my ear. "Nobody wants you in that thong."

"You being Nobody?" I asked right as he slipped the panties down my legs.

"Exactly."

CHAPTER TWENTY-ONE

"Hey, babe, you okay?" Tuck asked me as I walked out of my last final.

We'd made it to the end of our senior year and never rotated out of each other's arms.

"I'm going to lie down," I said pushing through the pain I had been fighting for the last hour.

Suddenly the pain in my gut had me curling into a ball.

"That's it. I'm taking you in."

"No, I'll go to the bathroom and be—Mother of God." I tried to stand up only to have the pain shoot down my legs making me tighten.

"Katie, you have a fever and are all clammy." His hands curled around my face.

"My sugar is good."

"And?"

"If I was really sick—"

"You want me to hurt you."

Tuck carried me to my car and laid me in the front seat letting the back down so I could stay curled in the fetal position. He drove slowly choosing to swerve to avoid any bumps and actually slowly stopping.

Pulling up to the door he rushed into the hospital and got people to help me out of the car. Snapping at them to be careful when he saw me wince.

They took my blood and realized I couldn't get up to give them a urine sample even though I felt like my bladder was about to burst. Then it was off to ultrasound where I had the most painful experience I had ever known.

While the drugs were making it so I could finally stretch out a little. Tuck's fingers ran through my hair while he leaned close to my head apologizing for not being able to take away the pain.

"Ms. Gills, we are going to need to send you to surgery." The doctor's cold voice caught me off guard.

"Surgery? Why?"

"It appears that you have what is called an ectopic pregnancy. This pain's been here for a few days?" he asked while pressing firmly on my left side making me screech.

"Pregnant?" Tuck's face blanched. "You're pregnant?"

"Actually, she was pregnant, but in this case the baby didn't go far enough down into her uterus so she is in serious condition. The baby's stuck in her fallopian tube and if it's not removed it could kill her."

"Are you sure?" I asked, even though I knew better. "There's no way to save it?"

"No. Right now we need to get you to the OR."

It seemed as if my whole world caved on me and I didn't even know what was going on. A baby. Tuck's baby was now killing me, or I killed it because I wasn't strong enough to hold it and keep it safe.

A whirl of action spun around me. Nurses and techs came in and out of the room. Checking my IV and administering drugs to course though my veins making the blur of people worse. I nodded when I understood a question, but Tuck's hand stayed wrapped around mine. We were both in a state of shock.

"Katie, I need you to count backward from a hundred."

"100, 99, 98…" I looked for Tuck, but he was gone now. I was alone in the cold sterile operating room. "97, 96—"

Soft shuffling sounds surrounded me as I felt as if I was walking through a tunnel to come back around.

"Tuck…" My throat burned, but I needed to know he was still here for me. "Tuck…"

"Hey, there, you waking up?"

The smell of cleaning alcohol hit me as I felt a soft hand brush my forehead. My eyes fluttered until I could make out a nurse on either side of an arm still blocking my view. She couldn't be more than a year older than me.

"I need you to sit up and I have some water for you."

I tried, but the pain was still there. So I dropped back down,

"Okay. It's okay. The doctor will be here soon."

"Is Tuck around?"

"Tuck?"

"Gus Tuckman he's—"

"There's a big black guy in the waiting room."

"That's him."

"I can go get him for you if you're up for it." I nodded even though I was afraid he'd be upset with me. How couldn't he? "Your father was called, and he said he'd be here probably in the next hour or so."

"Thanks."

I turned to look at the frayed pale blue and green curtains and it was then I realized that I had blood going into my IV as well as saline. The room was a single, but with all the monitors hooked up to me I wondered if I was in the ICU. How bad had it gotten? Was it not just a simple miscarriage? Not that any miscarriage was simple, but something had to have gone wrong.

Footsteps made me turn back to the door and I saw the outline of Tuck from the dim light of the hallway. His frame filling the opening and creating a halo around him. What made my heart ache was he seemed to fear stepping in the room.

"I'm sorry," I said.

"For what?"

"I lost your baby. I didn't even know…"

"It wasn't your fault."

"I wasn't strong enough. Or built right…"

"Hey, we don't know what happened."

"You almost killed my daughter!" My dad's strong voice powered through the room as he pushed past Tuck. "I want you out of here and out of her life."

"Dad."

"No. This has gone on long enough. Tuck, your irresponsible behavior endangered her life. Only immediate family is allowed in the ICU."

"Dad, please. I was just as culpable…"

It was then that the room spun again, and the fog took over. The monitors that had been silent alarmed waking up the sleeping ward. My father stood over me until the physician in charge of my care arrived then it was a free for all.

At least that's what I thought happened, but it could have all been a dream or nightmare. It seemed like those three days moving from ICU to a regular floor to the dorm acted that way. I tried calling Tuck when my father wasn't around, but he didn't answer.

Not only had I lost the small piece of him growing inside of me, but he seemed to have disappeared too. The doctors assured me that I would still be able to have children. They had removed the baby before permanent damage or tearing occurred, but I still couldn't focus on anything.

I lay in my room on my futon just staring at the pictures of me and Tuck. The blurred images remained fuzzy as I tried to find a place to grab on to, but I couldn't. I was floating in a world that was only real when I felt a stab of pain or my father tried to shake me out of it.

"It's a good thing, Katie. Abortions happen when there is something that is wrong with the fetus. You would have had a child with disabilities, or some sort of disorder had it gone to term."

"Abortion? I didn't have an abortion. Was my baby alive when they took it out?"

"The correct medical term is spontaneous abortion. I raised you better than that. You do not get attached to the patient or confuse the vernacular because of popular language."

"The patient? I was the patient. How do I not attach to me?"

"You know what I mean. You had a procedure that naturally comes with complications. You survived and are completely healed from a medical standpoint."

"Where's Tuck?"

"I've taken care of him."

"How have you taken care of him?"

"I told him it is not healthy for you two to be together. This is as good a time as any to make a clean break. Graduation's tomorrow then you're off to medical school."

"I don't want a break."

"Katherine Alice, you don't know what's best for you."

"And you do? I've done everything you've asked—"

"I didn't ask for you to be a knocked-up whore. How could you have started medical school pregnant?"

"I don't want to go to medical school." I did, but he didn't need to know that. Because right now I was so confused I needed a rock to center me.

"What are you going to do?"

"I don't know, but it's not school. It's not this. Just go. Go away."

"I've taken time off until you graduate. I took one of the parents rooms in the basement so I'm staying."

"Why? To keep me away from Tuck?"

"Among other things. I got you early admission to Northwestern. You'll start in three weeks and you'll be ahead of your class. The last thing you need is this little hiccup to throw your whole schedule off."

"It wasn't a hiccup, it was my child. I can't be here right now. I need to leave."

Finding my keys I took off for the lobby and ran across the courtyard to the men's dorm.

"Page Gus Tuckman please," I asked the guy working the desk who was thrilled as ever to be reading his Latin American history book.

"Gus Tuckman," he said as he depressed the button. "Gus Tuckman."

"Yes."

"You have a visitor." The silence on the other end of the intercom made my heart cave in on itself. The cheap plastic clock on the wall thundered with every tick of the second hand.

"I'll be down." To me it had been an hour, but the desk clerk didn't seem to notice.

"Hey."

I wanted to run into his arms. I needed to feel them around me, but he just stood holding open the fire door for me to walk through.

"Tuck…"

"Not yet." We walked in silence to his room without touching. His room was half empty and I didn't understand what was going on.

"Are you leaving?"

"After graduation."

"Right, that's in two days."

"I got an apartment."

"What's going on? Is this it? This is how it ends? I'm sorry. I didn't mean to get pregnant. It was an accident I swear."

"I'm not mad about you getting pregnant." He couldn't look at me. He wouldn't turn. "I don't want it to end, but I've been made aware that I'm not supposed to be with you."

"Hold me. Please, Tuck. We both lost our baby. I need someone to hold me and tell me they still love me. Even if it's a lie."

His arms wrapped around me and I felt as if I could disappear in them. The burning in my throat made it hard to breathe and the reality of losing him was becoming too great.

"I'll always love you. You're mine, right?"

"Yes. And you're mine. Tuck, screw my father. It's me not him."

"Leave with me. I found an apartment in town. I've got a job lined up. Come on. Move in with me."

"Okay, I will."

"Really? Did your dad tell you he's taking away your trust if you don't go to medical school?"

"No. And what does that have to do with anything?"

"You're willing to live on Ramen and tuna fish?"

"Not in the same meal, but with you. Yes."

He pulled back and finally I saw him again. Not this guy who was so cold and unfeeling.

"They told me you almost died."

"I heard."

"I did that?"

"How?"

"I got you pregnant."

"I was there too. I want to spend the night here."

"I want you to."

Curling into Tuck's chest I could finally breathe again. My dad had taught me to distance myself. I hadn't cried yet. But in that moment, I finally realized what I had lost, and I finally cried for my baby. Tuck held me and rocked me to sleep as I sobbed. His hand stroking my hair as he whispered, *I know baby, I know.*

CHAPTER TWENTY-TWO

I woke up and knew what I had to do. Writing two letters to the men in my life. To my father I told him to pack up whatever was in my room and take it home. Keep it in the garage or a storage unit, but I would be back for it someday.

To Tuck it was harder.

Tuck,

I need time and space right now. I want to be with you, but I need to be with myself right now. What can I say? You were warned I was selfish and spoiled. I'm also a child because I can't say this to your face. I'm going on a journey, but I will return in the fall. Meet me at the Alumni mixer for homecoming. I'll be ready for whatever you have to offer me. Don't call because I won't answer, but you know me I never miss a deadline. So meet me there.

Please do not think that my leaving is in anyway a reflection of my love for you. I'll always be yours Tuck, but right now I need to find out who or what I am so that I can fully be yours. It's four months Tuck. Four months and I'll be back.

I love you.

Kate

I placed the sheet of notebook paper on his pillow as I softly kissed his head. Creeping out of the dorm I went back to my room and placed my father's note on my dresser. I pulled out three bags and filled them with clothes, books and my pictures of Tuck and me. Then I grabbed my basket and threw whatever else I thought I'd want. Computer, DVDs, iPod.

There's no need to cross a stage to graduate. I filled up my car and took off in the middle of the night heading southeast. I didn't know where I was going or what I'd find when I got there, but I needed this to find out who I was and what I truly wanted. Because outside of Tuck, I had no idea.

The sun rose and for the first time I saw the beauty in it. Pulling off on a scenic outlook I sat along a cliff over a river watching the world as it woke up and relaxed. Part of me was trying to say I should be doing this with Tuck, but I've always been my father's daughter and now Tuck's girl. I've never been me. As scared as I was to take this chance, I had the GPS that Tuck gave me. I know it will always bring me back to him and keep me safe.

Breathing in the fresh air I remembered being lost as a child. Tuck was right, I hadn't been lost I was exploring the world, that was the last time it hadn't frightened me. When the sun was up, I headed out in search of a diner. The GPS would be the quickest method, but I knew this had to be an exploration not a guided tour. That was my safety net.

My phone flashed notifying me I had at least one message. Scrolling through my phone log there were fifteen calls from Tuck. Each a minute apart. My father had made one. That would be my warning call. And it appears Mark's up too.

Before I took off, I suppose I should listen. Swallowing hard the computerized voice told me I had six messages.

"Katie, pick up." Tuck's voice was firm. *"Please don't do this. Come back now."*

"I thought you didn't want to end it."

"Katherine, you have school starting in three weeks. I will not be

placing additional funds in your accounts or release your trust until I hear from the provost that you have started class."

Delete.

"Katie, baby, please call me. We can't work this out if we're not talking." This isn't what I wanted. It wasn't him. It was me.

"Hey, Katie, am I on your do-not-call list?" Mark sounded confused. "Tuck's here. He just told me. I'm sorry, I know you didn't plan it, but would you have left if the baby hadn't happened? If not, then you shouldn't have left."

"Katie, Tuck's gone. Call me, please. I'm worried about you. He's really angry. Do you want me to try to smooth it over? I can't do that if you don't call. This can't be what you want. You may have lost him."

I saved all of Tuck's messages and deleted the rest. Pulling out of the parking area I decided I should at least call Mark.

"Is Tuck there?"

"No. Why didn't you call him?"

"Because I'd turn around and run back to him if I talked to him."

"And that's bad why?"

I didn't know. I didn't know why I left. I didn't know how to put it in words.

"Katie do you want to be with him?"

"Yes."

"Why didn't you come to my room and talk instead of taking off for who knows where?"

"Something's missing and I think it's me. I've never been able to define myself without attaching someone else to me."

"I have," Mark offered.

"Who am I then?"

"My best friend who will kill to protect me."

I sighed and gazed down the road.

"Do you want me to tell him anything?"

"That I love him and if he still loves me, he'll see me at Homecoming."

"Where are you going?"

"I'll see you later, okay?"

"Katie—"

"I won't call you again. Not until homecoming. I may need a room to crash in."

"I'll be here. I don't know how I'm going to get through senior year without you."

"You aren't me. You never needed anyone to lean on. Love you, Mark."

"Love you, too."

———

"Can I get you anything else, Sugar?" the waitress asked as a black man walked behind her and kissed her on the cheek.

"They were fresh out of good bananas." His love for her obvious in his dark eyes.

"Did you get the rotten ones?" she asked.

"No."

"I told you the ones that are almost spoiled make the best bread."

"I'm sorry. I didn't want you to die from food poisoning."

"Since when?" she joked back at him then turned back around to me.

"Is that your husband?" I asked.

"For the last seventeen years whether he wants to admit it or not," she yelled back toward the kitchen.

"Oh, shut up you old wind bag."

"Jackass."

I had to laugh at their banter.

"Why? You don't think we should be married?"

"It's not that, isn't it hard sometimes?"

"To be with a jackass? Yes. Or to be with a black man?"

"The second part." She slid into the other side of the booth and stared at me.

"Every man is hard to be with. For me it's harder to breathe when he's not around. It's like there's air everywhere, but I can't pull it in. Even when he's gone to the store a part of me isn't here. I wasn't going to let society's rules take away the only part of me that ever felt right. You let it, didn't you?"

"I don't know. I'm a little lost right now."

"You won't be found until you get him back. Our bodies are just a package. Some have pretty bows, and some got roughed up in the transport. It what's inside that package makes you complete that's all that matter. Or are you somebody that likes to play with a box then put it out for recycling at the end of the week?"

"That was me, before him."

"He feel the same?"

"Let's just say we met on recycling day and decided that we couldn't leave the other on the curb."

"Why are you here, Sugar?"

"I've never done anything on my own. Always afraid. He helped me gain my strength."

"Then you left him? Have you ever thought how that made him feel?"

My head landed on my crossed arms resting on the table. "I fucked up again."

"Maybe? Maybe not." She patted my head. "How about a piece of pie for breakfast?"

A half hour later I was back on the road hopping on highways that made sense, not really knowing where I was going to end up. Every part of me was lost so all I could do was pray I'd turn the right way in the end.

CHAPTER TWENTY-THREE

Walking into my sister's clinic all the bright colors adorning the walls of the Pediatric Orthopedic Center greeted me. There were cartoon characters with crutches painted on either side of the door and bright flowers indicating summertime on the windows. In the courtyard area there was a set of benches circling a statue of a fairy sprite water fountain.

All in all a serene place to come if you needed a break from whatever goes on inside.

Entering the lobby I saw a red, green, blue and yellow waiting room with kids in casts playing with bead trays, trucks and dolls. Some parents were reading stories from books that showed the years of use being held together by tape in some spots.

The plump woman behind the front desk smiled at me as I approached. Her hair was pulled back into a bun and she wore Mickey Mouse scrubs.

"Can I help you?"

"I'm Katherine Gills, Dr. Gills' sister."

"Oh, hello, I should have known from the eyes."

I never understood the instant connection. People always seemed compelled to connect family members by some genetic trait.

Kimberly's mother was tall and lean with blond hair. She takes after her where I take after our father.

"Could you please tell her I'm out here?"

"Absolutely."

Watching children playing I sat in a hard-backed chair. There was a baby in a carrier that must have been born with a club foot or something. His poor tiny body had casts on each leg.

"Katherine Gills," A nurse called as she stepped out into the lobby and I stood. "This way please."

Following the woman a bit confused for a moment until I realized my sister wouldn't come into the lobby for fear of her patients mobbing her with 'quick' questions.

Sitting down in her office I saw her degrees on the wall and a picture of her and my father at graduation. Nothing more personal.

"Katie." Her stern voice caught me off guard. "Why are you here? And why didn't you call?"

"Last minute decision."

She crossed to her chair and sat behind her desk. Her eyes upset with me for inconveniencing her.

"Last minute?" I could tell by her tone she did not approve. "I have two more patients today then we can go out to eat I suppose."

"Okay."

"You can wait here until I'm done. We can discuss your decision at dinner."

Somehow, I traveled fifteen hundred miles away from my father and still ended up with him. I should leave.

"It's good to see you, Katherine," she said as she gently touched my shoulder on her way out.

Forty minutes later Kimberly drove us to a restaurant, but as we pulled up her beeper went off.

"Damn it. I'm on call for fifteen more minutes."

Knowing what my father would have done, ignore the first page because a second page would go out to his partner in twenty minutes when call rotated, I was a bit surprised by my sister. Kimberly pulled out her phone and called the service then called the hospital.

"Are both the radius and ulna involved? A huh. So greenstick on ulna, but the radius broke through the skin? And there is no joint involvement? How? Never mind. Yes, I'll come in. If nothing else I'm extremely curious how that's physically possible." She hung up and looked at me.

"Curiosity killed the cat."

"But his satisfaction brought him back," she replied surprising the hell out me. "Do you mind? I can push it off to my partner." There was a sparkle in her eyes making me think deep down she was human.

"No. Come on how many times have I entertained myself in an ER? I'll be fine. It does sound interesting."

"Doesn't it." She smiled so big I wondered if her whole body was tingling as she explained what the ER doctor had told her about the patient. Her detailed teaching of the bone structure had me appreciating her expertise. If nothing else I know who to go to with bone questions.

"Kimber, my dear." A younger doctor swooned as we walked through the ER.

His long white coat had his name embroidered in blue right above his left pocket. *Charles Morter M.D. Emergency Medicine*. He sported a short buzz haircut probably to avoid his receding hairline. About the same height as Kimberly's five nine, with a lean build, still the standard ceil blue hospital scrubs did show a little muscle definition.

"Dr. Gills," she snapped, and he coughed pulling up the x-ray images on his computer.

"See here?" He pointed to the wrist. "Somehow, she lucked out and broke about a half an inch above the wrist."

"Yes. I see." She leaned in closer then pulled back. "What about this?" she asked pointing to the bone.

"What?" he asked, clearly not seeing what she saw.

"Does she have cancer in her history?"

"No. What are you—" The recognition hit his face like a ton of bricks. "That's why that bone snapped so easily. I was so interested in the injury—"

"You didn't look for its root cause. That bone is riddled with cancer. How it hasn't spread to the ulna is the medical mystery. How old?"

"Eight."

She turned to me then back to him.

"Dr. Morter, can you please do me a favor. My sister arrived unexpectedly this afternoon." The hard gaze was the same look my father gave me when he'd pawn me off to one of his nurses. "She's starting med school in the fall so could you let her shadow you while I take care of this patient? Toss her in a short white or something. I'm going to have to use the C-arm to set the fracture. Can you have someone contact x-ray to set it up?"

"Sure." He turned smiling at me. "You can call me Chuck."

"Dr. Morter is the preferred deference," my sister corrected. "What room is the patient in?"

"Sixteen," Chuck grumbled and passed my sister the chart. "Come with me, Padawan Gills," he snipped at me.

Poor guy was probably thinking he'd been stuck with another cold fish like my sister.

"Katie," I corrected

"Huh?"

"My name is Katie, Chuck."

He smiled as he walked me to the doctor's lounge. "Has Dr. Gills always been that tightly wrapped or was it med school that did it?"

"It's genetic," I informed him as he passed me a short white coat indicating med student. "I had someone help me remove the stick from my ass."

"Was it a long procedure?"

"Yes. Painful at times."

"Your patients will thank you later. Being a doctor isn't about playing God. It's about fighting his angels. Let me tell you a secret."

I leaned in close.

"They love a sense of humor. I'm serious when I need to be, but you put people at ease by dropping to their level. Plus you have to choose to laugh or cry. The criers rarely make it."

"Avoiding attachment."

"That the genetic disorder?" he stated.

"You like my sister, don't you?"

"I'm a glutton for punishment."

"I've known too many of those."

"You going to tell me how to break the ice queen?"

"I'll give you a number for the guy who melted me."

"Now, I'm interested. Where is he?"

My eyes instantly stung as tears bit the edges of my eyes. "Long story."

"They're never that long, junior ice princess."

Crossing my arms, I swallowed back the ache from leaving Tuck and sighed. Chuck followed suit letting me know I wouldn't get away with holding it in and I realized, although Tuck had held me and let me cry, I hadn't processed what had happened in a larger sense. I'd never see Chuck again so what did it matter if I talked to him.

"For graduation, I had an ectopic," I stated with a slight crack in my voice.

"Oh." Instantly sympathy filled his eyes.

"I had complications and was in the ICU for a few days. I don't really remember much."

"What did he do?"

"Not much. My father wouldn't allow him near me, and I was so out of it I couldn't protest. I'm not sure what was said to him, but until I was released from the hospital, I didn't see him."

"When you saw him what happened?"

"He held me all night and let me cry. Asked me to move in with him."

"That scared you and you ran away?"

"No. It comforted me and let me know that he'd always be there for me."

"So you talked to him before you left?"

"Too chicken. I needed to figure out who I am. I've always been afraid to do anything. He made me strong, but I felt like my strength was dependent on him not because he unleashed something within me. Now I'm thinking I screwed up. I asked him to meet me at homecoming in October then we could start our life together."

"What happens if he doesn't?"

"Then I'm screwed."

"Is he a glutton like me?"

"We've been together for almost two years."

"He'll be there," he assured, placing his hand on my shoulder.

"You ever felt like a failure?"

"Everyday."

"But you're a doctor?"

"Why do you think they call it practice? We can't be right a hundred percent of the time."

"You haven't met my father."

"Anything like your sister?"

"I thought so, but she actually took the page you sent."

"Let's go." He led me into a room. "Hello, Ms. Dawson, I have a medical student with me today. Would you mind if she observed?"

"Well, I don't—"

"I promise I won't let her do anything, but the major procedures. I hate doing those. The simple stuff I can do in my sleep. Usually, I do." The patient laughed then nodded her head yes. "Okay, so I see here you had your prostrate removed?" he joked. "No, seriously, how long has the ringing been in your ears?" he asked, sincerely.

We went through a few more rooms as he let me press on the

patients' stomachs to feel the impacted colon, look in the throats to see the strep, showed me the rhythm strips to see the A-fib then we walked into Mrs. Lucas' room.

She was laying on her back with her eyes locked on a spot on the wall. Her mouth was open like she was trying to say something but got stuck.

"Mrs. Lucas has a positive O sign. Do you know what that his?" Chuck asked softly.

"No."

"Her mouth. What does that instantly tell you about the patient?"

"She doesn't have dentures in."

He laughed. "That too. She's more than likely a dementia patient that had an abnormal lab and was sent by the nursing home. This is Florida. We have a lot of positive O signs around here. Mrs. Lucas my name is Dr. Morter I'm going to be taking care of you today." He raised his voice, but she didn't respond. "I see here that Dr. Zaminski sent you in because you appear to have a bladder infection. We're going to give you some medicine and we should be able to send you back to the nursing home tonight."

She kept her head turned and didn't respond. He did his H and P like he had with all the rest of the patients, answering his questions with her chart instead of her responses. When we left the room, I was more confused.

"Why did you do that?"

"What? Talk to her like a human."

I nodded, embarrassed at my question.

"Look, her mind passed on, but her body didn't get the message. Sometimes the mind travels back into the body and I get a response. I don't know if her soul has passed on or if it's just trapped. But if you were trapped in a dark room would you be able to find your way out if someone talked to you and gave you an anchor?"

"I guess."

"They are all human. Not case studies. Behind every x-ray and lab report is a real live person with a heart and soul."

"Our father teaches us separation. No attachments."

"How's that worked for you?"

Glancing at my feet my stomach tightened.

"When you were in the hospital how were you treated?"

"My father told me I needed to separate from the patient."

Chuck shook his head in disbelief.

"I now understand Kimber better." I tilted my head surprised at his candor for her name. "Excuse me. I understand Dr. Gills better."

"Tell me how you practice?"

"I have ten to fifteen minutes to assess and fix a patient. I have to gain their trust. How do you do that in such a short amount of time?"

"Some people have that ability without even trying."

"Let me guess. The one who melted you?"

"Very much so."

"Attachments happen. Unhealthy attachments are the problem. I lose patients every day. Florida is called God's waiting room for a reason. But I choose to look at what that person brought me in those few minutes or hours they were with me. Maybe I learned something new, like with your sister's patient. Maybe I saw a glimmer of thanks as I let someone pass on. I used to get frustrated when I lost a patient until a nurse said are you upset at losing the battle or losing the human?

"Katie, I don't know if it's the right or the wrong way to look at things but going into medicine isn't like any other family business. Just because your father or sister do it doesn't mean you should. Medicine is a noble profession with a lot of fuck ups in it."

A smile pulled at the corner of my lips.

"And they aren't the ones who screw up patient care. They're the ones that don't care for the patient. Humans are like snowflakes. Each different and beautiful."

A morbidly obese patient was rolled by making us both turn to see this man with fat hanging off the sides of the stretcher being pushed by two people. A room filled up with techs and nurses to move him over to an ER bed.

"Beautiful is the wrong word. Unique and special. Do you know how I avoid the burn out?"

"Alcohol and Class A narcotics?"

He laughed.

"Maybe you can be a doctor, smart ass. I'm the jokester around here. Keep your sense of humor. You'll need it. If you don't, you'll cry out of frustration."

"I don't cry."

"What about when you lost your child?"

Until I felt Tuck's arms around me again, I was numb, silent, absent of even my own consciousness. His deep voice telling me everything would be okay. I shook myself from the memory, but it was too late. Chuck saw my weakness.

"Did you see any interesting cases?" my sister asked as she foamed her hands with disinfectant even though she had probably done it a thousand times since she left her patient.

"A few."

"Did you actually teach her something or were you just trying to get her undressed the whole time?"

"We copulated in the doctor's lounge to get that out of the way and then focused on the patients," I said keeping my face straight as if I was giving a report on the patient's status. "I found it satisfying if not amateurish in his insistence on me saying 'that's not a speculum'."

My sister stared at me in shock then turned to Chuck who burst out laughing.

"Are you sure you two are related? Katie please go to the University of Miami. I so want you as my resident."

"Katherine will be a surgeon like the rest of my family," Kimberly informed him. "Have you picked your specialty yet?"

"Colorectal seems to be in high demand lately," I replied then winked at Chuck who burst out in laughter again.

CHAPTER TWENTY-FOUR

"Would you mind if we ate at my house?" Kimberly asked as we walked out of the hospital. "I have some leftovers."

"That's fine."

We drove to her condo. It was exactly what I expected. Two bedrooms with an open kitchen leading to the dining area then the living room. The granite countertops were high quality. Not that I expected anything less. My father had won his home in the first divorce from Kimberly and Kenneth's mother. She had impeccable and expensive taste. Obviously, Kimberly had inherited that.

The jen-air stove with its open gas burners and stainless steel oven reminded me of the crappy one in the basement of the dorm. All those cookies. I turned and sat on a gray leather stool she had at by her breakfast bar.

A few pieces of contemporary art were hanging in the room. Black and white photos of surgical equipment. But then there was one that used landmarks to spell out the word HOME that took me by surprise.

She pulled out a few cartons of left over Chinese and smelled the containers.

"They're from last night. I've got fried rice, chicken and pea pods, sesame chicken and a few egg rolls. What do you want?"

"All of that for just you?"

"I need to tell you something."

"You're seeing someone." I smiled.

"I'm married. I don't want it to get out." She reached above the sink to a small dish and pulled out a wedding band. It was platinum with five inlaid diamonds. If the diamonds weren't so big, I'd have thought it was an anniversary band.

"You're married? Did I even get an invitation?"

"No one knows. If you wouldn't have shown up today, you still wouldn't have known."

"Why is it so bad to let people know?"

I hadn't heard the door so the male voice startled me.

"That's my question," Chuck said as he turned the corner and saddled up behind Kimberly his hands landing on her hips. She was dishing out the dinners onto plates as he kissed her gently on her neck. "Honey, you cooked." His voice hitting an octave higher than normal. "You shouldn't have."

I had to laugh.

"Yes, she's making me chicken and pea pods," I said, letting her know my choice.

"You are special," he joked as he reached into the same dish pulling out a matching platinum band except, he had a rectangular shaped diamond that seemed to cover the top of his finger. "I think she doesn't tell anyone so she can let the interns hit on her. She has such an ego."

Kimberly smacked his ass with her spoon then tossed it in the sink.

"So what was the wedding like?"

"City hall. Only witness was the county clerk," Chuck grumbled.

"You haven't even told your mother?"

I had always been jealous of Kimberly for having a mother around, even if her mother was a male version of our father.

"Tell me about your mother. Kimber doesn't talk about anyone in the family."

"Well…we're all in witness protection."

"I got that."

"Her mother—"

"Her mother?" Chuck questioned.

"Our father believes in monogamy. He's a serial monogamist. Kimberly's from the first round. I'm from the third. He's currently looking for round five."

I could see Chuck calculating up what I had just thrown out to him. "Hmmm got it, I think."

"I'm going to change since you insist on being a gossip," Kimberly said leaving the room and Chuck elbowed me.

"Spill it all. If I'm going to get in trouble it might as well be worth it." The microwave dinged and he brought me my plate then put his in. The buttons beeped as he programmed it then sat back down by me.

I blew on the chicken then took a bite only to see him with his head resting on the palms of his hands.

"Okay so you and Kimber share a father."

"Right. My father has five children. Kimberly has a twin brother Kenneth—"

Chuck cut me off. "She's a twin!"

"You've got to be kidding me," I said aghast. Tuck knew everything about me, and Kimberly hadn't given her own husband the smallest detail about her. "I need to up my ice queen policies. I thought I had tough rules."

"Your man knows about you, doesn't he?"

"She's wishy-washy like her mother," Kimberly returned snapping at me. "That's why she killed herself. She let her emotions get the better of her."

"Apologize now," Chuck ordered Kimberly who was crossing the room. "That is your sister. Stop being like this, Kimber. You've got to stop it."

Pain burned in Chuck's eyes, but what he didn't realize was I was raised with my siblings attacking me about my mother. The weak one.

Maybe it was because my father raised Kyle and me while they all were raised by their mothers, angry hateful ones.

"I'm used to it," I said in her defense. The sadness in my voice caught me off guard.

"She is gone, and it was her decision to leave. There is nothing left in that body. Both of you need to stop trying to place meaning on something that isn't there."

"Daddy, we want to go to her grave."

"Kyle there is nothing there but a headstone. A waste of money if you ask me."

I turned away from the memory and saw that Chuck's worry wasn't about me.

"I've learned more about why you are the way you are in the last few hours then in our whole marriage. I love you, Kimber, but your skill with those children has to translate to the rest of the world."

My sister's face showed her receding back to someplace safe. Someplace in the back of her mind where she played music or recited the bones in the human hand. Anyplace where she didn't have to deal with the world around her and feel what was right on the surface. Chuck turned to me to try to explain.

"Katie, you should see her with her patients. It's like a whole different person, then she turns to the parents and this is what I get. I'll apologize for her behavior since she refuses to be the person buried deep inside."

"Kimberly's mother is like our father. Attachment's not allowed. I assume she's better with children because they attach without malice in their heart. There is no refusal especially when it comes to the youngest among them."

"Quit trying to run your undergrad psych class bullshit on me," Kimberly snarled.

"When I was younger, and it was her weekend she'd sneak into my room and take care of me. Especially after my mother died."

"I did not."

"As I got older, she distanced herself from me. I never knew why. Guess I was more judgmental."

"I was in college."

"You were still who I wanted to be like. It's not like I ever had a female role model."

"Are you two fighting?" Chuck interjected. "I've never seen anyone fight without showing emotion. Are you guys sociopaths?"

We both turned in unison and scoffed at him.

"You are related and it's not only the grey eyes."

"Why do people always look for a genetic trait?" I whined.

"Tell me about it. Yes, genetically the five of us got our father's eye color. So does a percentage of the population."

"You have four siblings?"

"She actually has seven," I said then spoke through a mouthful of food. "Her mother had two more children with her second husband."

"You're going to get TMJ the way you flap your gums."

"I thought it came from grinding your teeth?" I teased.

"Then you're going to get it," Chuck pointed out to Kimberly while shoving an egg roll in his mouth. "You're going to need to tell soon."

"No," Kimber snapped.

"Why?" I smiled.

"We're having a baby." Chuck beamed.

"It's none of their business."

"You want me to start the rumor you're a lesbian who did a freezer pop baby?"

Kimberly looked at Chuck and softened. Who would want to deny him the pride he was feeling of getting her pregnant? He loved her and wanted to tell the world about the expression of love. Her hand slid across her abdomen in protection. Drumming her fingers she dropped her head.

"No," she replied softly.

"It's funny. I thought the only good gossip about you was that you smoked pot."

Kimberly's head shot up. "Who told you that?"

"You smoked pot?" Chuck bellowed. "Kimber we're having your family over more often."

"No, we're not. Tell me who said that."

"Don't smoke with Kyle if you don't want the world to know." Winking I scooped up another bite.

"Who's Kyle?"

"Our brother."

"It was like five years ago," Kimberly said dropping her head into her hands.

"Okay, that's it I'm getting a dry-erase board and you're going to draw a family tree."

"Wait, I got a better idea," I said sliding off the stool and digging through her cupboards. "Is this a bachelor pad? Give it up, lady, I know you've got the goods," I joked. Kimberly was the one who taught me to make cookies and I knew she'd have the supplies on hand.

Kimberly smiled at me and started to pull out the kitchen utensils I need. Together we started to bake the cookies. Chuck sat back and watched as we measured each part every part of the recipes we both had memorized. One batch of oatmeal raisin, one of chocolate chip and one cinnamon.

"Your mother taught me," Kimberly explained spooning the dough onto the cookie sheet. "That's why I thought you'd like to learn."

"Have you ever broken down Dad's marriages?" I asked. Kimberly shrugged her shoulders and opened the oven. "Think about it. Your mother is him, but he wanted someone to mother him not be his equal."

"So that's why he married Joan?"

"And Joan would be?" Chuck asked.

"Joan is Kevin's mother. She's almost smothering with how loving she is."

"That's why Kevin does what he does," I said.

"What does he do?"

"Doctors Without Borders. He's in Rwanda?" I questioned and glanced at Kimberly for confirmation. She was the mother of our little brood.

"Actually he talked Kenneth into going to Russia."

"Why Russia?"

"HBO did a special on the *Chernobyl Heart*. When he saw this kid needed a butterfly valve, but it cost more than the cardiologist made in a year there, he talked Ken into performing a few surgeries."

"How often do you get together as a family?" Chuck questioned.

"Well, I'd say at weddings…"

Kimberly smacked me.

"It's been years. We talk once in a while," Kimberly said nonchalantly, but I could see the shock in Chuck's eyes. Tuck had the same disgusted expression when I said you don't show up without calling ahead.

"You want me to blow your mind?" I asked and Chuck nodded. "We never visit the other without a phone call to make sure it's okay. I crossed a line this afternoon."

"It was quite inappropriate to show up like that."

"She's had a hard month," Chuck said placing his hand on mine and squeezing.

"How's that? Finals aren't devastating."

"I should have known Dad wouldn't have called you. I lost a baby. Was in the ICU for a few days due to complications. Almost died. Ring any bells? Didn't think so."

"You know how to use birth control, right?"

No sympathy, instead, Kimberly was checking off my failure.

"It's not a hundred percent," I said in my defense.

"Who was the father?"

"My boyfriend," I replied as a chill cut through me thinking about Tuck.

"Where's he?" Kimberly asked.

"Still in Cassen, I think."

"You don't know?" The condemnation was starting.

"I left him to get my head on straight."

"You let him knock you off track," Kimberly scolded with the stern cold grey eyes I'd feared my whole life.

"She fell in love," Chuck interjected. "You know the feeling, right."

"Stop," Kimberly ordered.

"You're lucky I'm into S and M. You gonna spank me later?"

Chuck stuck a fork full of food in his mouth.

"Isn't she pretty when she's mad, Katie?" he teased out of the corner of his mouth once he swallowed and Kimberly had turned a perfectly bright red.

"She's pretty all the time."

The timer went off and I turned to take out the cookies. When I turned around Kimberly was in Chuck's arms accepting an apologetic kiss. I saw her lips mouth the words 'I love you' and Chuck nodded like he knew all the time.

Kimberly spun back around and appeared embarrassed.

"You guys are adorable," I said, and Kimberly smiled.

"Not that I haven't enjoyed the fact that you are making cookies, but what does this have to do with the family tree" Chuck reached for a warm one only to be smacked by a spatula.

"We really need a few more kinds of cookies. Oh, well." I started breaking apart the cookies keeping the chocolate chip ones. The constant. "You have the twins. Kimberly and Kenneth Jr. Then we have Kyle."

"Find the softest cookie for him."

"Meany. He is the softest," I admitted.

Then I started putting the pieces together.

"Chocolate chip is our father," I stated breaking three cookies in half. "You don't have any store brands, do you?"

"Why?"

"Conner, Ella, Luke, Patty and Sadie."

"Oh, maybe," Kimberly said digging through her cupboards. "I got fudge stripes and soft batch."

"Do you confuse easily?" I asked and Chuck laughed.

"I'm still confused but pass me a cookie." The half of a chocolate chip I didn't need I passed to him.

Laying out our family tree was fun. My dad the chocolate chip, Kimberly's mom the soft batch since they were so alike making up Kimberly and Kenneth. Then half a chocolate chip, half oatmeal raisin made up Kevin. Finally half chocolate chip half cinnamon for Kyle and me. Then I broke up a few more for Conner and Ella, Kimberly's siblings from her mom's side, with the soft batch and fudge stripes. And for Luke, Patty and Sadie I had to use Oatmeal and fudge stripes.

"I think I got it. But these three…"

"Luke, Patty, and Sadie."

"Right. They don't have the same father. You just needed some *Nila Wafers* or something right?"

"Yeah." I cocked my head sideways and observed my confectionary family tree and had to smile.

"What are you planning to do, Katie?" Kimberly asked.

"For the first time in my life I don't know," I answered honestly. "How does one find themselves?"

"Ask me in the morning, I have clinic so I'm going to crash." With a light peck to Chuck's cheek she said her goodnights. "Put the cookies away. You've had enough, Katherine."

I stuck my tongue out. Kimberly shook her head and went into the bedroom.

"Being on your own is overrated," Chuck said. "Most times you find out about yourself from the reflection others give of you."

"You think I should turn around and go back?"

"Nope, didn't say that. Offering a perspective. You observe the world. I saw that today. Now I need you to step back even farther and interpret what you see." Chuck yawned and stretched. "I'll see you in the morning, or not. This is your journey to take. Remember that if it doesn't end the way you want it to."

CHAPTER TWENTY-FIVE

I'm officially stuck on the couch. On Demand had become my best friend and I think I'd been watching way too much *South Park*. *Give me my damn cheezie poofs* had become my catch phrase. I even learned to like turkey pot pies.

Homecoming had come and gone with no sign of Tuck. No message he would be there two days late or even telling me to fuck off. Instead, nothing.

It's not that Mark didn't have another bed, but the thought I wasn't laying in bed all day meant I wasn't completely destroyed. Deluding myself had become my favorite pastime.

I'm not sure what day it was because I'd completely lost track of time. It was a weekday though because soap operas were on. The People's Court should be on soon. Stretching out my arms I reached above my head as my toes pointed into a perfect pirouette.

Mark's key turned in the lock and I rolled on my side.

"Good morning, sunshine. I see you've gotten your daily supply of dairy today," Mark snipped so I threw a cheezie poof at him. "Nice."

"My head hurts. Leave me alone."

Dropping his backpack at the door he slowly walked over to the couch and lifted my feet placing them on his lap. Slapping his hand hard on my ass made me scream and roll over to my back.

"Jerk."

"That's it. Fight me all you want but this has to be done."

"What has to be done?"

"This." Mark stood up then grabbed me, throwing me over his shoulder, ass high, like a damn sack of potatoes.

"Clifton Marcus," I yelled, punching his back.

"Stuff it, Katherine," he snapped, and slapped my ass again as he walked me kicking and screaming to the bathroom. "It's been two weeks. I can handle the depression, the permanent indent on my couch and the increase in your starch intake, but the smell, Katie—the smell would gag a maggot."

"Screw you." I heard the water come on and hit against the porcelain tub. "You wouldn't—ahhhhhh," I screamed as he put me in the shower fully clothed.

Each attempt I made to move got me shoved back in. I was too tired to fight him. Instead, I crumbled to the tub and curled into a ball. The sobbing started sometime when Mark was scrubbing my hair to get a good lather.

"Why am I so stupid? Why? All I had to do was stay with him that morning. Or turn back around. Or call him. Why, Mark? Why can't I let myself be happy?"

He didn't answer. Instead, he removed the showerhead from its hook and rinsed my hair. Allowing his fingers to catch in the tangles. My body shook and when I lifted my head, I saw Mark holding back tears.

"I'm going to strip you down now. Can I add music?" he joked as he pulled off my t-shirt only to have me scream again and cover my chest. "I'm sorry," he said, embarrassed, and finally stopping the assault with soap and water. "I should have known you didn't have a bra on."

"What does it matter anyway?" I asked defeated by the situation as my hands fell from lack of muscle control.

"Can you take it from here? I mean if I leave you alone would you actually clean yourself?"

"Maybe?"

"Hey, it's better than what I'd thought you'd say." He lightly kissed my forehead then pulled the shower curtain closed. I didn't hear the door though.

"Are you sitting on the toilet?"

"I'm not takin' a deuce if that's what you're asking."

"Leave, please," I said as I stood, stripped off my pants and socks tossing them over the curtain bar. They landed with a plop and grunt from Mark.

"Well, now that you're naked…"

"Get out."

"I'm getting, I'm getting."

———

Wrapping the towel around my chest I walked out into the apartment to see Mark resting on his bed reading his Organic Chem book.

"You should have taken that with me," I said.

"Tell me something I don't know," he replied as his blue highlighter ran over the text.

Crawling on his bed I curled up next to him and started to play with his hair. Strangely I wanted to get closer to him and when I was about to undo the towel his hand found mine.

"No."

"Come on, lets try again."

"I know I'll regret this tomorrow, but no."

"Don't you want to be the guy to—"

"To what? Fuck you while you cry the whole time because I'm not him. Gee, where can I sign up for that?"

I flopped back on his bed and started to pout crossing my arms and twitching my feet. He was right though. I was trying to push Tuck out of my mind and even the thought of sex with anyone, but him made me start to cry. Mark stayed focused on his book pissing me off more because I needed him to hold me. Couldn't he understand that?

After about ten minutes of silent tears I started to get up only to have him grab me by the waist and start to spoon with me.

"You're my best friend. I'll do anything for you." He paused as his chin rested on my shoulder. "Well, almost anything. Really I don't want to embarrass myself being at half mast all the time as I try not to think about the fact that it's you I'm inside."

"Gee, thanks. I never knew I was so repulsive."

"You know better than that."

"Whatever."

"Would that I could my lovely, but we both know you and I will always be the best of companions. Although when we get married at seventy thanks to a new little blue pill, I will be dicking you down like no one's business."

"And now I've gotta puke."

"You are such a tease. A minute ago you were going to ride me like a wild bucking bronco."

"Thank you for looking out for me. Do you think he'll take me back?"

"I don't know, sweetheart. Have you called him?"

"No. Maybe I should move on." Even as the words came out, I knew they were a lie. How could I move on from him?"

"So what now? You going to stay in Cassen and get a job? Or finally make that trip to Antarctica?"

"I want to go to medical school, just not Northwestern."

"I thought you didn't want to be a doctor," he said. I got up crossing to his dresser and pulling out one of his shirts.

"Well," I said as I pulled it over my head then dropped the towel. "How else can I use and abuse you if you're not my nurse?"

"That is true, but are you sure in your spiritual awakening that you in a long white coat is what you want? Or is it just all you know?"

"Can I borrow your plane?" I asked.

"You know most people ask to borrow a cup of sugar."

"I've got a cup of sugar."

"What do you want it for?"

"I think it's time to see Kevin."

"Charity work…oh I get it…you really want to piss off your father."

"No. I want to see what a real doctor can do."

"Where is he?" Mark asked.

"Last I heard Russia, but I think he was going to Darfur next so he may be there."

"Can you promise me my plane won't end up with holes in it?"

"No, but would you be my date?"

"You want to travel like thirty hours for a weekend jaunt?"

"What day is it?"

"Monday."

"Really?" I wondered how many Mondays had passed since Homecoming.

"I was with you on the couch for the last two days."

"Oh, yeah, right…well how about this, take Thursday and Friday off and we can leave Wednesday night. That way I can firm up where he's at."

"Fine, then what?" Mark asked tossing his textbook on his nightstand.

"Then can I have your penthouse until I get into med school?"

Crossing his arms, he let out a long sigh. "Why don't you just call him instead of running away again?"

"What if he says no?"

"What if he says yes?"

"I told him how to come to me."

"And the world revolves around Katherine Gills' rules." Mark stood and brushed back my wet hair.

"He knew," I croaked, trying to push past the hard lump in my throat. "He knew I'd be there, and he didn't come."

"A thousand things could have happened and if you don't call him, you'll never know."

"What if one of those things is he found another woman? One with less baggage and a positive outlook on life."

"You know you can have the second one."

Could I really? Did I, when I was with Tuck, the world seemed open and yet shut in a way.

CHAPTER TWENTY-SIX

Entering the back of the lecture hall I saw an open seat by the door. Sliding in the seat I clutched the table of the desk and tried to disappear. Without Tuck by my side I'd returned to the invisible girl. Even my father didn't notice me.

"When would surgical intervention be called for with ulcerative colitis?"

A few hands went up. One with an embarrassing urgency and I feared I was seeing a mirror image of myself. Although the medical student was male, I couldn't help thinking that's how I was in class in need of constant approval of my knowledge. Almost jumping out of his seat. God, did I look that stupid? My father overlooked all of them finding another student cowering in the corner.

"Ms. Lesser," his condescending tone sent a chill down my spine. Her fingers started to turn the pages of her textbook in some desperate attempt to hit the right page in time. "Ms. Lesser, has anyone in your family succeeded at anything?"

"Yes, Dr. Gills. You didn't assign—"

"At the beginning of the semester did you not get a syllabus?"

"Yes, sir."

"The syllabus covered everything we will address this semester. I never said when we'd cover them. So you were to be prepared the whole semester. If you would have attended over half my lectures you would know that. Why are you wasting my time and your parents' money?"

"Failure to respond to traditional treatments leading to multiple hospitalizations," I said wanting to save this girl from my father's wrath.

"Who said that?" he barked turning toward where I was.

"Changes in the lining of the colon suggesting the patient is skewing toward cancer."

Now he saw me. "You're not a student here."

"Unlike your student. I know if the irritated bowel perforates then it is necessary for surgical intervention to remove the large colon and rectum. You then connect the small intestine to the anus."

"It's too bad you'll never be a doctor. It seems you have potential. Time students. I've been reminded to have you stop by the medical school administrative office to pick up your short whites. After the holiday you will be assigned to a resident."

The rest of the lecture hall grabbed their books and walked up the steps while I walked against the crowd meeting my father at the front podium.

"Guess you don't remember the wonder twins didn't start med school until they were twenty-three," I said, leaning on the podium looking at my father.

"I remember. Their mother—"

"Stop. I don't want to hear how this person failed or that person did this."

"Did you come home for the holiday? If so, I'll have to make some arrangements with Cynthia for dinner."

"Who's Cynthia?"

"The woman I've been seeing."

"I came to get my stuff. That is if you didn't put it all in the trash."

"You can't get your trust fund. That is unless you're planning on attending medical school. What are your plans for the future, Katherine? Run off with that man? Become a waitress? Tutor the underprivileged?"

"Whatever I decide you've made it clear I've crossed the Maginot line."

"Do not be overly dramatic because you made an error in judgment," he lectured picking up his briefcase and walking toward the exit.

I followed thinking our family was the least dramatic group I'd ever seen. Tuck's family got more animated discussing what was for dinner than my father ever got over his divorces.

"Your grandchild was an error in judgment?"

"Was it planned?"

"No," I replied and even I could hear the whine in my voice.

"Then it was an error in judgment."

"You ever had an error in judgment?' I asked not really wanting an answer.

"Katherine."

"Are you scolding me or telling me my place in the world of oops?"

"What do you want from me?"

"I hoped I could get my winter clothes. I know anything more than that is pushing it."

"I gave you and your siblings everything and what do I ask for in return?"

"Complete obedience."

"Please."

"What am I supposed to be?" I asked as he scoffed and crossed the parking ramp to his car. "A surgeon. Like my sister, brothers and father."

"Kevin is not a surgeon."

"Dad, you do realize I knew the answer to your question when I was ten. Quiz me. I guarantee I know more than most third-year med students."

"And you're throwing it away."

"How? Because I fell in love." The lump burning in my throat expanded to encase my heart caught in a vice.

"You don't know what love is."

"You do? When did you learn?"

"I'm going out tonight. Your property is in the extra stall of my garage. Leave your key on the counter."

"So that's it. I'm cut out of your life."

"I refuse to watch you fail."

"Who said I'm failing?" I turned to leave only to hear my father make one final plea.

"Kimberly said at one time you were interested in colorectal. You seem to have a predilection for it."

Her sister probably told him a nugget of information to pacify his need and avoid her own life. Well two can play that game.

"If I go to medical school, I won't be a surgeon. But answer me this. Is Kimberly's child an error in judgment?"

"Excuse me?"

"Due any day now. I wonder why she and her husband haven't told you." Okay so it wasn't my place to tell him, but damn it someone eventually will have to make him see that he's created a group of socially atypical monsters.

CHAPTER TWENTY-SEVEN

Thank God for maintenance men and rolling carts. Although I had to load my stuff myself, by the time I got to Mark's he had alerted his building and they were helpful. His grandmother chose to live along the North Shore of Chicago with access to the lake she never went on as opposed to Mark who enjoyed the view. Money could get you anything you ever wanted in life. The Hancock Building didn't have two story condos. Or they didn't before Mark purchased two full floors of condos and demoed the place.

A bonus came from the fact he could choose to get off the elevator at his bedroom level if he wanted. Either way, his home would be mine for the week followed by the long Chicago winter. My admission to Northwestern had been deferred, but I couldn't go to a school where my father taught. It would be a coup on his part. Once I was back from visiting Kevin, I would restart my search for schools and apply if I still wanted to go.

Once settled a bit, I ordered food and crashed in a chair hanging on a hook next to a window with a full view of the lake. A cat jumped up on my lap and I screamed.

"Who the hell are you?" I questioned the tabby more interested in curling against me instead of running away from the freaking out stranger. Thankfully, I'd grabbed Mark's phone before I sat down.

"All moved in, Katie?" he answered the phone.

"Why is there a cat in your house?"

"Because some people prefer having a live one to a dissected one."

"You don't live here."

"Yeah, but cats don't need much. I pay a girl to come in, play with her or him, feed the thing and clean its box."

"You have a cat you pay someone to play with?" I questioned as the thing began to purr in my lap.

"Well, I found it on the street one weekend. It wasn't chipped and the vet said it was malnourished."

"This isn't having a pet you know that, right?"

"My apartment here won't let me have an animal. When I come home, I'll take over duties. Speaking of which, your rent will be you playing with it."

"It has no name?"

"Lift its butt, check the sex and you can name it. Two holes it's a girl, one for a boy."

"No," I protested.

"How about Mitten's the Remix?"

"It has no mittens on its paws." My hand absently petted the damn thing. "You order those supplies to take to Darfur?"

"Am I an ATM to you?"

"You pay someone to play with your pet. As down to Earth as you say you are, that's not right."

"Fine, I'll have them loaded on the plane. Cargo alone will get us hijacked, you know that, right?"

"Fingers crossed. Then I can show my sweet moves."

"What are those?" he questioned. "Hitting the highest note a human can hear while peeing your pants."

"Got us out of your Grandmother's charity event didn't it?"

"Be on the plane Thursday night. They'll fly you here and I'll go with you under protest."

"Wouldn't have it any other way."

Lifting the cat I set it on the ground and extricated myself from the chair. This animal was obviously in need of attention because it followed me around enough with its tail in the air, I learned it was a girl.

"All right, Princess," I said as I made my way to the pantry and found the only food in the house. Wet cat food. I wondered if there was a crystal glass to feed old Princess out of. Cracking the can she mewed until I placed it on the floor. "Ghetto Princess?"

For the next few days I gathered medical supplies, toys and food. Even found a place with seed packs still available. The poor man tasked with bringing me to the private airstrip wasn't exactly sure how he was going to get all my items into his vehicle. Nothing better than having access to Mark's black card. He wouldn't notice a slight uptick in purchases. Besides, he hadn't had to pay Kira the cat sitter for a few days and when I came back because I would be in charge of Princess. Kira never gave me her name for the feline, but I thought I heard her grumble something like Dip Shit at one point.

Loaded for goodness and giving I buckled myself in and prepared for the long flight. Mark and I spoke for the first few hours as I began to fill out medical school applications. Just the basics, the essay would have to wait for inspiration. An inspiration that slammed into me less than an hour after landing in Africa.

CHAPTER TWENTY-EIGHT

Money has a way of smoothing out unmade plans. Maybe it was the months of driving with no real destination and living off what was in my pockets that turned me into a flighty wanderer. Or was it when the one plan I had fell apart that I realized planning was overrated? Either way, Mark wasn't exactly a fly by the seat of his pants guy, but he managed to arrange for transportation, an armed escort and got us to the tent hospital my brother was working out of.

"Katie?" Kevin questioned as he emerged from a tent with his hand blocking the sun above his eyes. "What the heck? Kimberly wrote that you showed up on her doorstep a few months ago, but this isn't exactly the place you pop in."

"Even if I brought presents?" I questioned while he rushed me into the tent and found Mark and I flak jackets.

"I wish you would have told me so I could have gotten you at the airport." Kevin's bright smile shone through all the dust, dirt and deeply tanned skin. "Wow, you're not my little sister anymore."

"Did you run the DNA and find out you were a pod person?" I joked.

"No, you're not a baby."

In Kevin's defense the last time he saw me I was in high school. More like starting high school.

"Is this Mark?" he questioned.

"Ever the sidekick."

"Hey, I'm more Batman in this case since it's my plane and money that got us here," Mark protested.

"How long are you here for?"

"Well the vacation package I purchased was only for the weekend," I joked. "Not that I have anything to rush back to, but my ride has class on Monday."

"Okay, well, I'm still on duty for a little bit."

"Can we help?" I asked. "Long flight got us antsy. Mark's almost a nurse and I know doctors by their given name."

"Dang you've grown into a smart ass. Sure, we're giving vaccines at the moment. You good at stabbing people?"

"I've been told I'm good with large barreled weaponry," Mark replied, and we helped by allowing another team to take a much needed break.

"Dr. Gills, Dr. Gills," a frantic man ran into the tent covered in blood.

"What is it?" Kevin replied, unfazed by the red covering the man's shirt and pants.

"A mother and child were attacked. I have others bringing them here. The bleeding, I couldn't—" The man's thick accent had me struggling to understand.

"Artan, they will get here, did you use the techniques I taught you?"

"Yes, sir, the pressure, the binding."

"Then we will care for them." My brother scanned the tent. "Katie, Mark, crash course in emergency medicine."

Ice ran in my veins. He didn't really expect Mark or I to attend to trauma victims. The soft grey of my brother's eyes told me the truth before he could speak the words.

"My nurses went to get a delivery, you're on deck."

Screams of the mother and small child bellowed over the people we'd been helping, speaking in a language I didn't understand.

"But—but—" I protested in vain.

Adrenaline spiked while we were being shoved into a curtained off area in the tent. A few gurneys were set up with clean linens soon turned red and brown before my eyes as a dust covered toddler was laid upon it.

My brother spoke to the mother in a mix of Sudanese and broken English. Mark passed me a pair of gloves and something snapped in me. The pressure dressing on the toddler's head was soaked through.

Head wounds bleed more than most areas. It doesn't mean there is a major injury. It could be a cut. Unwinding the torn rag from around the baby's head I found a four-inch gash cut down to the skull.

"I see bone," I called out to my brother. "Not sure if a major vessel is hit, but he's bled a lot. Belly is distended."

"That makes sense. His mother said he's been running a fever for days. Vomiting and diarrhea. She was bringing him here to be checked out when the Army came through."

Mark held the boy down as I rinsed the wound out.

"I know, little man," I murmured, trying to calm the screaming baby. "Not the way to start a day. We've got you."

My eyes finally made contact with the boy's. They blinked, with no tears.

"He's dehydrated," I said to Mark. "You can start an IV, right?"

"Depends on how dry he is. I'll try. Don't you think Kevin should?"

Glancing at my brother I shook my head. "Did you see the mother?"

"No, why?" Mark began to turn.

"Don't," I warned. "Her arm is hanging by a tendon."

"I didn't need to eat today anyway," he said retrieving an IV kit and bringing his forearm to his lips I assumed to hold in the vomit.

Shaking his head he focused on getting the IV as I reapplied the pressure dressing.

"How long before another doctor shows up? Or nurse?"

"Hey," Mark balked after successfully starting the IV.

"Fine, one that can legally do that."

"I wonder if I could get credit for this?" he said and began wiping down the kid.

"Legally I don't think you're allowed to do any of this," I said.

"Yeah, well, Artan didn't finish fifth grade and he's a pseudo paramedic around here," Kevin said as Artan helped him with the airway for the mother as she was knocked out. "In a pinch we adjust around here."

"Still, I've never sutured before."

"Has the bleeding stopped?" my brother questioned.

"Not really."

"Well, I'll assist you in stitching once I finish amputating mama's arm here. Not that they didn't do a bang up job already for me."

"Can't you save it?" I questioned.

"In theory…" he replied. "But with no follow up care and we can't even house a person for more than a few days it would more than likely become gangrenous and she'd become septic."

My brother sliced the last of the tendon and Artan put the lifeless arm on a table for later disposal. Cleaning and stitching Kevin created a skin flap at the end of the nub. Mark stayed focused on the younger patient.

"But," I questioned only to get Kevin shaking his head.

"Katie, there aren't the resources here. I wish there were, but right now we're about to be slammed."

"What do you mean?" I asked.

"These are the trickles before the dam bursts. The soldiers were going to war." He nodded to Artan and removed his gloves. "Take her to the recovery tent and watch her. We'll need you soon."

"Yes, Dr. Gills."

"Let's stitch up her baby and pray the other volunteers make it back before the rush."

Thirty-six hours later I was grateful for Mark's plane. Exhausted, dirty and unable to scrub myself clean we collapsed in the soft leather seats.

"There are millions of places you could have gone on vacation," Mark said. "Why do I have the feeling we were not properly vaccinated for this jaunt?"

"How does Kevin do it every day?" I wondered.

"Pretty sure Dr. Nuesbaum helps."

"Tanya? Wait, is he… that sneaky bastard."

"Doubt she's the only reason, but Katie, you know I'll be talking with my grandmother about what we witnessed."

"I really want to do this," I said. "Not there where I have to use a pallet as a cast because there isn't any more plaster, but the rush of trauma."

Mark didn't reply. He'd passed out completely. Although I should have been exhausted, I was invigorated. Retrieving my laptop I began typing about the experience for my application essay. Instead of touting my love for discovery and my want to be a doctor since before I could walk, like I had in the one for Northwestern, this time I found my true voice. The one screaming to come out had finally appeared. I was someone outside of my father's daughter or Tuck's woman. Katherine Gills had finally been found.

CHAPTER TWENTY-NINE

"Is it time for your yearly sabbatical that pisses you off?" Melody asked.

"It doesn't piss me off." It crushes me.

"Whatever, Doc. I hope I don't see you for a few weeks after."

"I'm not that bad." Okay, I was, but Melody was my favorite nurse and having to work here with the likes of Jim or Trudy was enough to start my depression early.

"Look, Kate, I don't know what you do when you go away, but it's not working so try something else. What's the definition of insanity?"

"Not listening to nurses that are smarter than you."

"Flattery will get you everywhere. But come on, skip it this year. Or I've got the weekend off so how about we hit the college clubs and find you a nice freshman that needs to learn about the way of the world."

"I can't," I said.

"Will the world explode if you don't go?"

"You figured it out. I'm a secret agent and if I don't go away the second weekend of October Armageddon will come down upon us. So, see, I can't not go."

"Give it up, Melody." Mark was back to the rescue.

Only he knew where I went to every year. Mark wrapped his arms around Mel's waist and rested his chin on her shoulder.

"Plus we're going out this weekend."

"See the M&M twins have a weekend of frivolity, before they're tied down forever."

"It's one baby." She smiled as Mark rubbed her belly.

"You made the mistake of having Mark be the father. Genetically it will come out as a pain in the ass."

"I'm pretty sure that's anatomically impossible." Melody smiled at Mark. "You just better be out of your funk by Halloween because you're delivering."

"I promise. This year I'll take Lexapro or Benzene to keep my smile on if my attempt to save the world is too much for me. But right now I need you to push some drugs on Mr. Yaroshi." I passed her the chart and went back to my computer to check the labs.

Mark stayed behind leaning against my desk. "Katie, please don't go. It's time to move on. What happened to the girl who lived with no regrets?"

"She screwed up."

"So *Google* him like a normal ex-girlfriend stalker. Try calling his old number but stop doing this."

"You don't understand, Mark, it has to be this way."

"What I don't understand is who you've become? You don't date, you don't have casual interludes, you work and sleep."

"I eat too."

"No, you don't. Lose two more pounds and I'm going to turn you in for being anorexic. Katie, you're my best friend and you have to stop falling apart like this. At some point you rebound."

"It was my fault."

"You're afraid. The great Katie Gills screwed up and you're afraid you'll do it again. Not everything is perfect."

"He was." I snatched a clipboard and headed in a room knowing full well Mark couldn't follow me. "Hello, Ms. Shanny, I'm Dr. Gills, what brought you in today?"

"My stomach. I've been throwing up, but my side is killing me." I saw her curled on her right side and reviewed the triage notes. UPT was negative, fever 103.6, heart rate elevated.

"Okay let's have you lie back. Are you able to do that? Any diarrhea or is it just nausea?"

Her face winced as she laid back but was still slightly tucked in on the right side.

"Both."

I pressed on the left side and saw her twitch slightly.

Moving to her belly button she screamed even though I only pushed slightly on her.

"Does the pain stay centralized or does it go up, down, left, right?"

"Right." Her face was pained.

"How many days has the pain been like this?"

"This bad since this morning I've been throwing up for two days."

"Okay, here's what I'm thinking. I need to get some labs run and a CT that you'll have to drink a liquid called contrast. It tastes terrible, but we'll mix it with apple juice. Any questions?"

"What is it?"

"Contrast allows us to get a better picture of the inside of you."

"No. What do I have?"

Here's my problem. I'm 99% sure of what she has, but I'm not allowed to tell her that as a certainty. I have to dance around it even though I know. Having the empirical evidence is necessary from a legal standpoint not a human one.

"I'm not sure right now but it looks like appendicitis, yet I need to have that verified before we move forward."

Now the patient started to panic. "Surgery. I'm going to be cut open?"

"Calm down. I didn't say that. I said it was a possibility and now we can do a laparoscopic procedure that is minimally invasive to remove your appendix as long as we get it diagnosed in time." I breathed in deep, pushing my father out and remembered my fear as a patient. Surrounding her hand in mine I sat down on the rolling stool so I wasn't standing over her. "Ms. Shanny, there is no reason to think the worst. Right now you have a bellyache and nothing more. It could be anything, but based on what I see now I think that the most likely cause is an inflamed appendix. Now if I'm wrong the worst thing that will happen is you drink some contrast. What's the thing that scares you the most?"

"Surgery."

"What about surgery is so unsettling?"

"I'm unconscious. They could leave stuff in me, take out the wrong thing, what if I don't wake up? What if I feel everything and can't speak?"

"Loss of control?"

"Yes."

"In the ER I have to gain trust quickly. In fifteen minutes you put your life in my hands. How ridiculous is our system?"

She smiled and I could feel the pulse in her wrist slowing down.

"Unfortunately, I can't see you for months and build that up, but have you ever had someone in the first moment they come into your life a warm blanket of safety surrounds you?"

"I guess."

"Pretend I'm them. Because the only thing I want is to stop your pain and take care of you." She laid back and started to breathe normal. I stood and placed my hand on her shoulder. "I'll be back after your results come in and we won't make one step without your complete understanding and approval. You're in control of this situation. I'm just here to offer my opinion based on my training."

Going back to my desk I saw Mark hadn't moved.

"Don't start. I got a hot appy in there that I need to get started. Hey, Tracy, can you please start a line and get some contrast into room three?"

"Katie…"

"Dr. Gills," I corrected letting him know I wasn't in the mood.

"Dr. Gills, you remind me of another stubborn doctor with the same name."

"Do not compare me to him."

"Then stop acting like him."

"I'm not."

"I don't want to see you crushed again. He's gone. Admit it."

"This is my Christmas. This is my chance for a miracle. Please don't tell me there isn't a Santa Claus."

"Make this be the last year."

"I can't promise that. Now, do you mind? I have to let Dr. Sandlow know what I have so my orders will go through."

Mark's arms surrounded me and hugged hard. "You're my oldest friend."

"Then you understand my neuroses."

"Freud, Maslow, and Adler couldn't figure out your neuroses. You want me to tag along? I graduated too, you know."

"You did? I thought I just snuck you on staff with a degree I printed off the internet."

"That's because I graduated with a degree in underwater basket weaving."

"Oh, yeah, I remember. Are you going to let me go?"

"Nope. You're—"

"Don't! Say! It!" Mark pulled away and I could see the hurt in his eyes. It wasn't from me hurting him, but because he knew he almost hurt me. "I've gotta go."

"Me too, my lunch break is almost over. Maybe next time you won't hog my wife with patients."

"Sorry, she's a real nurse not a floor nurse."

"One of these days I'll start an IV and give a Tylenol and you'll know the truth about my skills."

"Kate, you're starting my IV, right?" Melody had returned.

"Yes, but if you don't get him off my back it'll be an IO."

Melody blanched, knowing I mean it. I would drill directly into her bone marrow and start a drip.

"Mark, leave now or I'm going to name your son Lucifer so God will know it's yours."

"You see that as a threat," Mark joked heading back to his floor.

CHAPTER THIRTY

T he swizzle sticks curved around and knotted nicely. Curling to create a head and legs.

"You still do that?" It was him. He came. Tuck's voice had been gone from my life for half a decade and still the moment he spoke I knew it was him.

"Only when I'm nervous."

"Or bored." He pulled out the folding chair next to me and sat. His hand took my drink and sipped it. I couldn't bring myself to look at him yet. His thick fingers curled around my glass was enough to start my body trembling in remembrance of when they held me. "Shirley Temple? Is there anything about you that has changed?"

"You're late."

"Am I? The party's just starting."

"I said homecoming 2000."

"Actually, you just said see you at homecoming. Maybe if you would have called me to firm up the plans I would have showed up."

"Where have you been?" I growled.

"Germany. After you left, I got a call from some guy from *NFL Europe*. Played there for a few years and yourself?"

"Here. I've been at every Homecoming for the last six years."

"Besides sitting here what have you been doing, drama queen?"

"Med school. I'm a first-year resident."

"In what?"

"ER. Couldn't decide."

"You in the ER? That must be a sight."

"I'm actually pretty good."

"Never a doubt," he replied.

"Are you still playing?" I asked, wrapping a second swizzle stick around my finger.

"No. I'm a psychologist."

"That seems right. Tuck?"

"Yes."

"There's something I need to say, and I need you to not interrupt."

"Okay. I'm better at that now."

"I fucked up."

There was no other way to say it. With every thought in my head that was the only one that made sense. And just to prove how much I fucked up I turned to him and saw the deep brown eyes that used to make my world right. Breathing in deep I held back my emotions so I could make my thoughts clear.

"Unlike most of my fuck ups, people saw it. You saw it."

My leg was bouncing under the table as I tried to look him in the eye, but I wasn't there yet. I may never be, but I had to let him know that I was the reason we ended. Part of me wondered if he even cared that we were over. Maybe he already had his closure.

"Do you know you put salt in a batch of cookies instead of baking soda once?" he asked stroking back my hair. "You were distracted and frustrated. I never thought you were perfect. At least not by anyone's standards but mine."

"That's impossible."

"It may be, but they failed, and you tossed them because you couldn't figure out why they didn't bake right."

"I'm sorry I left—sorry's not the right word. I was upset and overwhelmed. I drove everywhere for about four months until homecoming then I came back and I prayed so hard that you'd be here." I glanced at him, but still couldn't keep my eyes on him so I turned back to the floor. "I regret not asking you to come with me. Everywhere I went there was something missing. At first, I thought it was me that was absent. It was like I was there, but I wasn't. Physically, yes, but without you there I was nothing. And since the moment I left I've regretted it. I know I have no right to ask for forgiveness and I'm sure there were a thousand ways I could have searched you out, but I thought if you came here then maybe a piece of you didn't hate me."

His hand stroked mine as my tears fell landing on top.

"Tuck, I'd have come back every year until I die and said the same thing. Please give me another chance. I haven't been with anyone or wanted anyone. You're the only person I want to spend time with."

"I need food. Can you get me some?" A very pregnant woman had arrived and placed her hand on Tuck's shoulder. Turning my head I wiped away my tears.

"Rashel, this is my friend, Katie." Tuck introduced me and then stood. "Don't leave, Katie, I want to finish this conversation."

Rashel sat with her round belly as big as a basketball. Her hair was cut short like a pixie with tired, but sparkling eyes. A soft yellow top flowed down her stomach where her hands were rubbing her belly with a large diamond on her left hand.

"How far along are you?"

"Seven months, three weeks, five days. Not that I'm counting.," she joked, but instead of humor my chest tightened.

"I better head out," I said. "I'm going to take off early tomorrow."

"You're not staying for the game tomorrow?"

"Not this year."

She cut her eyes at me accusingly. "Where do you live?"

"Columbia, Missouri."

"And you drove here for this gathering and that's it?"

She wasn't buying it and I could see Tuck was halfway through the food line.

"Gus wanted you to stay here."

"I can't stay."

"You're *that* Katie, aren't you?"

"It was nice meeting you. Tell him I said goodbye."

"Don't you think you should say it for yourself once?"

I took off for the parking lot. My chest ached as I passed all the places on campus filled with memories of him. My Tuck. My man. The last thing I needed was his pregnant wife lecturing me. The stupid unlock button was not working on my keypad. I kept pushing and pushing, but the lights just wouldn't flicker.

"Katie! Katie! Come back here."

"No," I cried.

"Don't do this again," he snapped, grabbed me and spun me around as I fell back against my car. "Why did you leave the first time?"

"Please, Tuck, let me go."

"Answer me. You said you've grown up. Prove it. You ran away."

Fear triggered, shaking my body. The streetlights were forming stars because my eyes were filled with tears.

"Go back to your wife."

"Wife? Katie, tell me why you left."

"Why didn't you come back?" I howled in pain. The pain of my mistake, my loss and knowing I'd failed in the only important test in my life. "I promised I'd be here."

"I was mad and out of the country. I could have come back, but you broke my heart. I was already crushed but you…" His hand made a fist and he turned punching a tree. "Why didn't you at least say goodbye to my face?"

"It would have taken one please, Katie, and I would have changed my mind. Hell, you kissing me when you woke up would have changed my mind."

"Then you never should have left."

"Don't you think I know that! I never played into stupid sappy romance crap till you came along. Then I took it too damn far."

"Why did you really leave? You weren't looking for some dumb romantic kiss in the rain reunion."

"Losing the baby was too much for me to process. It made me realized I could lose you."

"That doesn't even make sense."

"I told you I was scared. Two years of having people call me names only to lose the baby. Do you know people said it was because I wasn't supposed to be with a black man? It was confirming that some higher power was against you and me. Now look, you have a beautiful black woman carrying your baby. She didn't lose it."

"Oh, Katie." His hand stroked back my hair as his hand supported my head that seemed to feel like it weighed a thousand pounds.

"Something easy seemed like the way to go, but not having you around made me realize I don't want easy I wanted what made me happy. Now it's too late."

"You never let me give you my graduation gift."

"Tuck…"

"It's been with me since you left." He dropped to one knee and held out a black velvet box that was worn on the edges like it had been rubbed a thousand times. Tuck flipped open the top to reveal an emerald cut diamond. "Katie Gills, will you marry me?"

"Your pregnant wife is in the damn Union and you ask me to marry you? Who the hell are you?"

"Rashel is Cedric's wife."

"Cedric's wife?" I croaked trying to find air.

"Cedric's wife. They live about five miles from my home in Cali. I was best man at his wedding."

"She's not having your baby?" The knot in my throat burned against my esophagus.

"God, I hope not. I don't think I've gotten that drunk at their house. You think I should call *Maury* just in case?"

"So you're not married?"

"Not yet, but if you're paying attention I'm trying to be."

"I hate you. You know that."

"Kinda got that impression."

"Why didn't you just tell me?"

"When did you give me a chance?"

"The moment she walked up."

"I finally got you back for Kyle." His head quirked to the side. "Look, it was a dirty thing to do, but Rashel hates you."

"I don't even know her."

"Yeah, but she's been trying to set me up for years only to have me complain that their eyes weren't right, they weren't fun enough, they didn't have a mental condition."

I laughed through my tears. "You want to marry me? After all these years?"

"I finally got permission."

"What?"

"Your father called me. He told me that the biggest mistake he made was when he told me I couldn't marry you."

"Why did you even ask?"

"I couldn't marry you without his blessing."

"And he gave it to you?"

"Yes. He said that for the last four years he's seen his daughter become so beautiful and happy at the beginning of October only to have her sink into a deep depression after the second weekend that lasts for almost twelve months. I was too hurt to try to come back the first year. Then I saw a picture with you in the background of the alumni notes and I knew. One captured moment of you in the stands and I knew."

"You talked to my father?"

"Do I need to repeat what he said?"

"I haven't talked to my father in five years. I picked up a few things from him then moved into Mark's place in Chicago."

"But you're in med school?"

"Because I wanted to be. My trust is sitting where it was when I left. Probably bigger because I went to med school, but I got in on my own. Got a scholarship. I wanted to do it on my own merits not his. So you don't have his permission. You'll never have his permission."

"So who called me?"

"Did he pay for your ticket here?"

"Mark. That explains why he said you don't date anyone, but implied sleeping with them."

"Yeah my dad would never know that about me."

"Why does your dad hate me?"

"You have a penis." I shook my head and finally looked at him. "I thought the same thing until Kimberly and I talked. It's not a black white thing, it's a daddy's little girl thing. I'll always love my father, but I got where I am today because of you. If you need his approval, then you might as well put that box away."

"Katie we both screwed up and were both miserable. I want my girl that still makes swizzle stick figures, drinks Shirley Temples and loves me. Is she still there?"

"Always."

"Then you're still the woman I fell in love with."

"I'm still yours?"

"Always. And I've always been yours. Say it. Come on, you know I want you to say it. Tuck, you are my—"

I grabbed his face and kissed him. It was like the last five years disappeared. My face still flushed. My heart still raced and every nerve in my body came alive. And for the first time in five years I could breathe again. At least I was sure when he stopped kissing me that I'd be able to breathe.

It wasn't easy, but it was better. Maybe I would have to fight if I truly wanted someone that made me who I wanted to be. No longer afraid of what was ahead of me, but eager for the chance to find out.

"Is that a yes?"

"It's always been yes. You never asked the question."

"One thing…." Tuck's words overtook me as he pulled back just enough to speak, but not enough to break our touch. "You have to wear an ankle bracelet because I can't have you leave me again."

"I don't repeat my mistakes. Promise."

"Promise."

ABOUT THE AUTHOR

Michel Prince is a USA Today best selling author who graduated with a bachelor degree in History and Political Science. Michel writes young adult and adult paranormal romance as well as contemporary romance.

With characters yelling "It's my turn, damn it!!!" She tries to explain to them that alas, she can only type a hundred and twenty words a minute and they will have wait their turn. She knows eventually they find their way out of her head and to her fingertips and she looks forward to sharing them with you.

When Michel can suppress the voices in her head she can be found at a scouting event or cheering for her son in a variety of sports. She would like to thank her family for always being in her corner, and especially her husband for supporting her every dream and never letting her give up.

Michel has been awarded Elite Status with Rebel Ink Press in 2013, the service award for her local RWA chapter Midwest Fiction Writers in 2013 and 2014, won Sweetest Romance at IREA and is a PAN member of RWA. She lives in the Twin Cities with her husband, son, and dogs, Bolt and Sawyer.

www.michelprincebooks.com
www.facebook.com/michelprincebooks
www.twitter.com/michelprince1

ALSO BY MICHEL PRINCE

The Growing Strong Series